WHIMSICAL OUTBREAK

THE MOST JOYFUL PLACE IN THE UNIVERSE 1

KAT CHARTIER

◆ FriesenPress

One Printers Way
Altona, MB R0G 0B0
Canada

www.friesenpress.com

ISBN
978-1-03-918433-6 (Hardcover)
978-1-03-918432-9 (Paperback)
978-1-03-918434-3 (eBook)

1. FICTION, HORROR

Distributed to the trade by The Ingram Book Company

Prologue

9:15 a.m.

"Just do it!" the older brother exclaims.

"No, you do it!" the younger brother replies.

Each of them goes back and forth before the elder of the two finally shoves his brother aside, calling him a pussy before leaning over the boat and staring down at his reflection in the questionably coloured water.

"Who's the pussy now?!" the younger brother taunts, noticing the hesitation.

With an agitated huff, the older boy reaches his arms into the water. He slowly cups his hands together under the murky liquid. Its touch cool to the skin and incredibly grimy to the touch. Definitely something not meant to be consumed by humans. Leaning over the boat's edge, the boy gazes at his hands in the water, disgusted not only by the water's unnatural feel and appearance but by the nauseating smell of chlorine combined with whatever unknown bodily fluids are mixed in. And just as he is about to chicken out, the boat makes a sharp turn on the track with a loud *thud*, startling the boy and triggering his reflexes. With no thought, he quickly pulls his hands out of the water and back in toward his face. As he sips the liquid, regret immediately takes over as he gags from the foul taste.

"You actually did it?" the younger brother exclaims with laughter and disbelief that his brother would do something so idiotic.

With a smirk on his face, as he is proud to show his brother he isn't a pussy, the older brother wipes his mouth with his arm. He leaves a long streak of blood, having not realized he cut himself on a track when the boat made its turn.

Had he just ingested the rusted metal, heavily chlorinated, with God knows what else was mixed in it, he would have probably just walked off the ride with an upset stomach, like every other person who did the challenge of drinking the water.

No one knows exactly what is in that water but, like venom, once it enters the bloodstream, it doesn't take long for the shit to hit the fan.

PART 1:
Whimsical Dominion

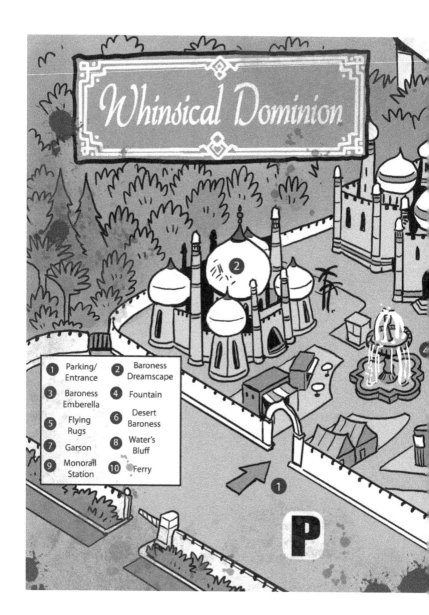

Chapter 1

t starts off as the perfect day.

The weather is a perfect seventy without a single cloud visible in the sky. Children scream with happiness while cheerful music plays in the background. The air is sickeningly sweet as the smells of candied apples and cotton candy waft through with the wind, leaving with hints of asphalt and sunscreen.

The most joyful place in the universe, a.k.a. Skippy World.

From the moment the gates open at nine o'clock in the morning, this is a world of endless waiting in line for rides, packed shops with overpriced souvenirs, and thousands of people eating questionable food prepared by greasy, zit-faced teens standing mindlessly behind deep fryers, wondering what unusual object they should toss into the fryer next.

Though the day has really just begun, Ray feels tired and is not really wanting to deal with lineups and crowds today, but, as much as he would like to just call it quits and go home, he knows he can't leave. Not yet. Not until his little one meets her hero.

At first glance, the lineup for the meet and greet doesn't seem so bad. With his daughter's little hand grasping Ray's hand tightly with overwhelming joy, they approach the end of the line. As it slowly moves a little, a sign is revealed.

"Two-hour wait from here," Ray reads to himself with a groan, contemplating if it might be best to just enjoy the park and come back another time. That is, till he glances down at his little one.

Bella, his beautiful daughter. The spitting image of his late wife, with her long brunette hair tied back into a somewhat messy braid. She has that look of innocence and wonder in her bright blue eyes as she calmly stands in the lineup beside her father. To Ray, they are standing in line for some underpaid teenager in a costume, but to his daughter, she is two hours away from meeting the most beautiful of all the baronesses: Emberella, the baroness of woodland creatures.

The one who spent her day cleaning and singing to animals while her stepfather lazily slept on the couch all day, lying in his own filth. Emberella had doubted that she'd ever be anything other than her father's maid. But one day, a handsome baron throws a magnificent party, and despite being told she can't go, Emberella sneaks out anyway and, well, you know the rest of the story.

As cliched as it is, Ray knows he can't back out now and risk disappointing his daughter. She's been waiting years for this moment, or at least since her late mother told her about the baroness' lore and explained that Emberella was who she was named after. Yep. In the debate on what to name their first child, Ray lost the battle, and because of it, his daughter probably had the same name as probably more than half the children running around the park. Hell, with no doubt, it's safe to say that most of the children whose parents grew up with Skippy World have unfortunately been named after some baron, baroness, or other property that had been consumed by the company that was rapidly buying the world. Ray feels bad for the kids stuck with the name Skippy . . .

Everyone has their favourite character, and Emberella was the baroness Ray's late wife grew up with. Naturally, she passed her love of Emberella on to his daughter.

"I wish Mommy can be here with us . . ." Bella says quietly as she gives Ray's hand a light squeeze.

Smiling softly, Ray returns the squeeze as his heart just breaks a little inside. She isn't wrong. "So do I."

An hour and a half passes, and like all other parents forced to wait in the lineup, Ray is exhausted from standing around and doing nothing. Thankfully, the end is near, and with just another thirty minutes' wait left, Baroness Emberella is in sight. A gorgeous young teenage girl with a red wig done up in French braids with some red ribbon weaved intricately through the braids. She has donned a large red and white ballgown with Emberella's signature crystal pumps, standing with a painted mural of her castle behind her and a red velvet rope that sections her off from the line, allowing the children a more intimate experience with the baroness.

It isn't long before the child just in front of Ray is just giving a tight hug to the baroness, finishing up his little meet and greet. As the boy runs back to his parents, the baroness gently raises her hand up, revealing a white bandage around her forearm that can't have been there very long. She elegantly waves at the young boy. Sweat beads along her forehead as her gentle wave transitions into a small brush against her face to wipe away the sweat. Her healthy, glowing skin pales as her breathing heavies.

Two staff members rush to Emberella's side, but she immediately brushes them off.

"Emberella can handle a little heat," the baroness says, keeping in character with a forced chuckle, before turning her attention to Ray's daughter, Bella, who is currently frozen in place at the front of the line. Behind her, like every other father, Ray is already crouched down with his phone held up and recording. He gives his daughter a little nudge with his elbow as he holds his phone as steady as possible.

The handler unhooks the velvet rope and gestures for Bella to come forward.

Finally, it is time for that magical moment.

"Go on," Ray whispers quietly to Bella as he records the moment.

Emberella crouches down to Bella's level and holds her arms out to call her over, noticing that the child is shy. Just when Ray thinks Bella can't get even more excited, somehow the little muscles in her face and the high-pitched squeal that escapes from her mouth prove him wrong. With the help of Ray's arm nudging her, she makes a break for it, running as fast as she can into Emberella's arms.

Ray knows that despite having to endure the heat of the sun, overpriced food, and endless walking and waiting in lines, this is a moment she is going to remember forever.

The sound of Bella's scream as teeth clench down into her carotid artery and the warm splatter of blood across his face will be the moment Ray remembers forever.

Chapter 2

Frozen in shock, Ray's mind plays that horrific moment on repeat. His daughter's bright, smiling young face, her warm embrace with Baroness Emberella, and the look of sheer terror as Emberella violently removes a large piece of flesh from her neck.

The baroness' two handlers immediately step into action, having been a little more alert as they had already separated a child from the baroness twenty minutes earlier. A child who had latched onto her arm with his own teeth. Of course, at that time, no one had thought anything of it, as children are unpredictable. They had got that child off Emberella (with only a small piece of her forearm missing); the parents stormed out with embarrassment that their child had behaved in such a way, and the actress playing Emberella was a good sport about it. She insisted a couple of bandages would be fine until her shift was over, as she knew how important these meet and greets are to people.

One handler, a somewhat built young male teenager, approaches Emberella from behind, wrapping his arms around the rabid baroness's chest in an attempt to restrain her while his female counterpart goes for Bella, trying to free her from the baroness' tight grasp. Naturally, when the young male grabs her, Emberella releases her hold on her current meal and whips herself around, trying to fight back against the teen on her back. This leaves Bella in the arms of an underpaid employee of Skippy World, who instinctively removes her work shirt and rolls it into a ball, pressing it hard against Bella's neck wound to try to stop the blood from spraying everywhere.

"Everyone, please remain calm!" a petite third handler calls out as she steps in front of the crowd, separating the patrons from the bloody scene with Baroness Emberella. "Please, just calmly evacuate the fortress in an orderly fashion!" she yells again, knowing that "child being eaten by actor" was not covered in her training. All she knows is that in the event of emergencies, there are evacuation protocols which she is going to follow.

Unfortunately, despite the efforts of the third handler, screams break out in the lineup. People shove each other as the situation turns into an *every man for themselves* scenario. Bloodcurdling screams echo through the fortress' hallways. A young man is shoved against the cold stone wall by his wife, who rips his ear off with her teeth. An old woman is shoved to the ground and trampled by panicking patrons in a confined hallway. A young girl, no older than six, tackles her older brother to the ground, and as her parents try to separate the two, she turns her attention to her mother, and immediately scratches out her mother's eye. The mother cries out in agony as she blindly takes a few steps backwards, tripping to the floor and meeting her demise as her head becomes the stomping ground of several panicked patrons.

Eyes now wild and lifeless, and with a nice chunk of bloodied flesh dangling from between her teeth, Emberella turns her attention to the teenage boy who is trying to pry her off the girl. With her head cocked to the side, Emberella opens her mouth, allowing the chunks of flesh between her teeth to fall to the ground before flinging herself on top of the handler.

The young handler screams out for help as her teeth connect with his face, piercing the flesh just under his eye. He tries to take a swing at the baroness with his right arm, only to find himself overpowered.

Emberella rips herself a nice large piece of face flesh before going in for more until the screaming fades and the handler's flailing comes to a halt.

As for the female handler who had failed in her attempt to save Bella, she is sitting there, cradling the young girl with her blood-soaked shirt still pressed firmly against Bella's neck, hoping that the park paramedics and police will arrive quickly. Crying and paralyzed with fear, she has no idea what to do.

Ray's attention is set on Emberella, who is currently making a snack out of a teenage boy. Ray is still completely frozen with shock and utterly oblivious to the chaos behind him. That is, until the crowd pushes a few patrons forward and into Ray, breaking him free from his frozen trance.

Stumbling a little, Ray looks around the room, trying

to piece together what is happening. People are yelling and pushing each other as they fight to get out of the fortress. Children are crying at the top of their lungs as their parents cover their eyes to try to spare them from the horrific scene unfurling all around them. Not that covering little Jimmy's eyes will protect him from the future trauma of the blood-curdling screams of people being eaten alive or trampled to death.

So much for an orderly evacuation.

Ray takes his attention away from the hysteric crowd, finally falling back onto his daughter. The one who was attacked by her hero, the one who is currently dead in the arms of a terrified girl who was probably just trying to save up for college.

"Bella!" he calls out as his heart pounds in his chest with horror, his mind finally catching up with what is happening. Processing and taking in every detail. Every moment of what transpired before him.

Shoving his way through the people trying to evacuate the building, Ray makes his way toward his daughter and the young girl. Quietly, he kneels down beside the girl, knowing she did her best. Hell, she didn't even have to do what she did. This is just an underpaid, overworked teenage girl who put her life at risk to save his daughter.

"You did everything you can," Ray says sympathetically, knowing that nothing can have been done. His heart rips in two at the moment. First, Maria had to be taken from him, and now his daughter? He was just trying to be a good father, doing the best he can to make his little girl happy, and now, here she is, lying lifeless with a gaping hole in her neck, in the arms of a girl that is probably no older than seventeen.

Ray places a hand on the handler's shoulder as he crouches down, tears rolling down his cheeks as he gently moves a strand of Bella's hair off her pale face. His chest feels tight as he is about to relieve the handler from the burden of holding his now-deceased daughter. However, just before he can take his daughter from the young girl, Bella's eyes shoot open, completely bloodshot and lacking any life. She gives a low moan, as if struggling to talk. The teenage girl and Ray are both shocked by what they are witnessing. Both of them are not prepared.

While most parents would stupidly get in their dead child's face only to succumb to a bloody fate, Ray is somewhat smarter than that. He knows from the moment his little Bella has half her throat torn out that she is dead. She is not coming back. Her life has literally been ripped away from her. While he is easing in closer to take his daughter from the teenage girl, Bella opens those dead, bloodshot eyes. That is the moment he realizes Bella is no longer his little girl. That is the moment his fight or flight instinct kicks in, and like a coward, he runs, not only leaving the innocent teenager who was trying to help his daughter through her demise, but abandoning his little girl. That is the moment, as he disappears into the crowd, that he fails as a father.

* * *

Bella arches her back, cracking the bones in her spine before thrusting herself forward. With her left hand, she violently grabs the teenage girl's arm, her nails digging into her arm like a cat digging its claws into its prey to prevent it from escaping.

The handler screams. She tries to pull her arm free from Bella, only to find that the more she struggles, the deeper into her skin the nails dig until blood breaks through the surface, streaming down her arm like a little red river.

Suddenly, Bella raises her head, opening her mouth wide, her pearly whites exposed as her jaw almost unhinges, almost tearing the corners of her lips.

Terrified, the teenage girl lets out one final shriek before Bella places her other hand on her face, her little fingers pressing firmly into the teenager's eyes until the tears that are already forming turn red as he nails pierce the cornea and continue through the iris. Bella then simultaneously pushes the handler's head toward the ground while her fingers burrow farther into the girl's eyes till she can feel the warm gooey centres, while tugging the girl's arm in the opposite direction until a loud *pop* is heard. The teenage girl's body falls limp, her eyes completely mutilated, concaved into the back of her skull as Bella holds her face like a bowling ball.

Even though the girl is no longer moving, Bella isn't finished. No. Holding the girl's dislocated arm up, Bella continues to rip the arm away from its body until the flesh connecting the shoulder and upper arm stretches and tears like an elastic band being stretched to its limits. With one final pull, the skin, tendons, veins, everything snaps, severing the arm.

As blood pools to the ground, staining the hardwood floors, Bella sits atop the teenage girl, taking a large bite out of her arm as though it is nothing more than an oversized chicken wing.

Chapter 3

When Ray entered the fortress with his little Bella, everything was normal. The cobblestone streets are clean, as the park was notorious for having its cleaning crew on alert at all times, there to practically catch any trash carelessly thrown away by people too damn lazy to look for the garbage bins before it hit the ground. The many stores are filling with parents ready to spend every dollar they had on cheap plastic trinkets, lame T-shirts that obnoxiously tell people you visited Skippy World, and cheesy-looking squirrel ear headbands. And though the lineups at the rides are well past the two-hour-long wait time, people still lined up. This is a place where families come together, adults get to be children again, and nothing else in the world matters.

Now, a young girl in a blue costume ballgown and a pair of pink squirrel ears approaches the balloon vendor located just outside Emberella's fortress and shyly requests a pink balloon. The over-enthusiastic vendor immediately reaches behind the little girl's ear, pretending there is a deflated pink balloon hidden behind the little girl's ear. She giggles. The helium tank lets out a quiet hiss as the pink balloon is placed over the nozzle and within seconds the little limp piece of rubber grows in a beautiful floating orb, reflecting the sun's light. It gently drifts above the girl like a fairy as the vendor lightly ties the balloon around the girl's wrist.

Beside the balloon vendor is a small stall that sells ice-cream with a never-ending lineup of children waiting with their parents to get a nice frozen treat. Apparently, in Skippy World, ice cream is alright to eat at nine in the morning.

Across the park, people are screaming. These are screams of joy, though. Screams that come from several of the park's rides and attractions. The most famous one in this particular park is a large water-log-themed ride known as Water's Bluff, a ride where a log filled with people floats upstream into some mountains only to descend a large hill and disappear into a wall of water. For those not wanting to get wet, there was Big Rumble Hill, a roller coaster that raced around a mountain that stood adjacent to Water's Bluff.

From stores, rides, fortresses, or street vendors, no matter which way you look, there is an overexcited hyperactive child who is barely being controlled by their exhausted-looking parents. The whole park is just an endless sea of children dressed up in pretty baroness dresses, wearing matching Skippy Squirrel/Shirley Squirrel ears while others are costumed as their favourite superheroes from the popular *Vindicators* movies.

Unfortunately, it doesn't take long for those joyful

screams to turn into screams of terror.

Balloons from the balloon vendor come loose and float away, disappearing one by one into the sky above as the balloon vendor runs from the children he had so happily played with.

The ice-cream stall is completely turned on its side. Vanilla ice-cream slowly melts against the sidewalk, creating a sticky white stream that eventually turns a dark pink as it mixes with puddles of blood. The employee who served the icy treats now becomes the treat as patrons young and old feast on his flesh.

Families who usually gather to pose for photos by the majestic fountain are now torn apart, literally. The fountain's once-clear, sparkling blue water is now tinted red and spraying into the air, filling it with the familiar scent of copper and death.

* * *

Baroness Dream Grace slowly makes her way through a screaming crowd of parents and children, each running for their lives. Dream Grace is the baroness known for not doing anything other than sleeping and still somehow she still managed to find love and have a happy ending. She is usually depicted as a kind and gorgeous woman with long blonde hair of silk and wearing a sleeveless, glimmering peach ballgown.

She passes by the majestic fountain, revealing that she is no longer the beauty for which she is known.

Her head is cocked to the side, her neck jagged where broken vertebrae pierce through the skin. Baroness Dream

Grace's signature blonde hair is now dyed with what we can only assume is the blood of her victims. Her dress is torn, shredded, and soaked in blood as part of her chest has been torn open, exposing her ribcage to the world.

The baroness grips the head of her enemy, Perilous, the spellcaster whose jealousy of Grace led Perilous to cast a sleeping spell on the baroness. Well . . . to be clear, it is actually the head of the employee cast to play the character.

Grace's hand grips the black hair of Perilous' head tightly, fingers tangled in the head's sticky, blood-soaked hair. With every step Grace takes, the head sways ever so slightly. The eyes wide open, forever staring ahead. Perilous' jaw is completely torn off, dangling by a small piece of skin, and revealing part of the spinal cord hanging from her neck. The head's expression forever fixed in time. A time that is filled with absolute terror the employee playing Perilous must have endured before meeting this horrific end. At least Dream Grace got the ending she deserved?

* * *

The young girl in the blue ballgown with the pink squirrel ears stands in the middle of the cobblestone streets. The balloon is still tied to her small wrist, frantically bouncing side to side as people run past her. She stands there, perfectly still, as if in her own little protective bubble, watching as the world around her falls apart from the inside. Quietly observing as her world of innocence and whimsy crumbles and people around her drop dead.

"Daisy!" an older woman calls out amid the crowd. A panicked mother who has lost her daughter in the crowd.

"Daisy!" she calls out once more, before spotting the young girl standing in a daze. "Oh, thank God!"

The mother hastily runs to her daughter from behind, pulling Daisy into a warm embrace. "I was so scared!" She breaks down in the tears, holding her daughter close. A clearly worried mother. Even without some sort of zombie outbreak, a lost child is a parent's number one nightmare.

The mother holds her daughter protectively, over-whelmed with emotion and uncertainty as to what is even happening. For a moment, the young girl's head is gently pressed against her mother's shoulder for comfort. The next moment, the little girl's blue dress is stained with blood as she sinks her teeth into her mother's throat. The woman who raised and loved her unconditionally. The woman who would love and accept her no matter what the future held for her falls to the ground, dead, blood pooling beside her as her daughter feasts upon her flesh. The world continues to move around them as the scene unfolds. Finally, the string tied around the little girl's wrist snaps, releasing the balloon into the sky above, slowly growing smaller and smaller as it disappears.

* * *

The joyous screams have been overpowered by screams of bloodcurdling terror and panic as people grab their kids and make a run toward the exit, where several overwhelmed workers try to control the crowd to get everyone out safely.

"Please, calm down! Form an orderly line!" one staff member calls out with a megaphone from atop a stool by the front gates as the funnelling crowd grows bigger.

Unfortunately, the efforts of the staff are in vain. People keep pushing and shoving, not caring who gets hurt in the process, as long as they themselves can get out alive. It is every man for themselves.

Completely backed up, with thousands of people trying to vacate the park, the large and vulnerable crowd of people attracts more and more undead patrons. It is hard to tell who is unluckier: those at the back, being jumped upon and mauled by undead children and adults, or those in the middle, getting pushed, trampled, and crushed, with nowhere to move as everyone becomes more panicked.

"Please, try to remain calm!" the staff member at the front calls out again. Just as he is about to speak once more, his ankle is gripped tightly. Before he can even react, he is yanked from below. He slips down, the stool flipping on his side as he falls.

Before the employee's body even hits the ground, his neck strikes the rim of the stool, breaking on impact and killing him instantly. Which is probably for the best as his body is dragged in close by an undead patron, who savagely begins ripping his flesh apart with his teeth.

* * *

Exiting the fortress, Ray watches in horror as bodies drop by the front gate. Some of those bodies get up and attack, while other bodies are too damaged to reanimate. It is clear that if anyone is going to get out of this place alive, it is not through the park's main exit. Any smart person would be able to clue into that.

Turning his attention away from the massacre at the

gates, Ray runs as fast as he humanly can, away from the massacre of people trying to flee the park. He weaves around the undead and continues past the countless bodies lining the blood-stained streets, making his way further into the park, unaware of what dangers lie ahead.

When Ray entered the fortress, everything was normal.

By the time Ray exits the fortress, everything has gone to shit.

Chapter 4

"Get back!" a frightened female voice cries out. The voice is coming from a woman no older than twenty-seven. She stands just outside the Flying Rugs ride, back pressed against the ride's fence, with two six-year-old boys held close to her.

Unlike most of the mothers visiting the park, who take appearances over comfort, she is wearing a green tank top, comfy capri pants, and, most importantly, running shoes. She knew she is in for a day of walking, and with two energetic boys, she has to be comfortable and is prepared for anything. Including an unprecedented zombie outbreak.

Behind her and the fence, the ride itself is still in motion. Ten cars in the shape of elegant rugs on the end of long poles, each at different heights, fly endlessly in a large circle while the ride attendant in his booth lays lifeless at the control panel.

A few feet in front of her, three undead patrons

approach, closing in on their prey. One male adult undead, who is slightly on the bigger side, wearing a newly torn (and bloodied) galactic space fight shirt, a petite undead woman wearing the iconic Shirley Squirrel ears with several bloodied bite marks on her body, and a smaller male undead child, wearing his favourite *Vindicators* costume, Metal Man. A family, most likely.

At first, the young mother protecting her children doesn't want to make any sudden movements; however, as the undead patrons get closer, she has no choice but to act. Turning her back on the group, she quickly lifts one child over the ride's fence, carefully lowering him to the ground, then immediately turns her attention back to child number two.

With the mother's sudden movement, the undead patrons pick up the pace. The patter of their steps grows faster and their groans get louder. With no time to waste, the young mother picks up her second child, her back fully turned and exposed to the approaching undead. Unlike with the first child, she doesn't have the luxury of gently placing him to the ground safely. She lifts the boy over the fence and drops him a few inches above the ground. As his balance isn't the best, he immediately lands on his knees. Almost instantly, tears form. There is no doubt that the mother feels bad for dropping him, but there is no time to waste. The mother firmly places her hands on the fence and uses it as support as she thrusts herself up into the air, leaping over to the other side. Good thing she frequents the gym several times a week.

The moment her feet touch the ground, she picks up her

crying child, holding him close while taking the wrist of her second child, running quickly and carefully through the queues toward the Flying Rugs.

With a loud thud, the three undead crash into the fence. While the two bigger undead cannot get past, it doesn't take long for the child to figure out it that there is a small gap between the fence and ground. A gap small enough that it can crawl under, and crawl under is what it does.

The young mother and her two boys make it to the front gate of the queue where the ride's entrance is, where and without hesitation, she opens up the gate and passes through, one child in her arms and the other still in tow.

Whoosh.

Whoosh.

Whoosh.

She is about to run into the middle, when one of the lower flying rugs swoops just inches away from the mother, stopping her dead in her tracks. Her eyes widen in horror at the thought that she has just about killed herself and kids, while trying to keep them from getting killed. Taking a quick moment to look back, she notices the undead child quickly making his way toward them, crawling on all fours like a rabid animal.

Unable to pass through the middle of the ride's enclosure to reach the exit, the young mother is left with no choice but to run along the ride's perimeter to reach the other side. Unfortunately for the young woman, running while holding one child and pulling another beside her, who clearly is struggling to keep up with his mother's pace, is not an easy task. Doesn't help either that during this chaos, the young boy's shoelace has come undone. As they approach the ride's exit, about to hop another fence, down goes the boy.

His hand slips from his mother's. Time slows. The woman glances back, seeing her son falling face first toward the ground. Not far behind him, the undead child is gaining. Closer and closer. She can hear her heart pounding through her chest as the world around her goes silent.

She horrified, as her son finally hits the ground and the undead child lets out a loud shriek as he grabs the boy's ankle, pulling him away from his mother's reach.

Chapter 5

As the woman runs through the gate with her children, entering the ride area, Ray's heart and conscience won't let him leave them. He has already started making his way toward the ride itself. Does he have a plan? No. He has no idea what he is doing or what he is going to do, but as the child trips and lets go of his mother's hand, Ray immediately hops the fence around the Flying Rugs ride.

Completely unarmed and without a plan, he considers all his options, which aren't much. All guns and potential weapons are confiscated at the park's entrance, which makes sense. There is no need for Second Amendment Steven to walk around a family park ready to shoot the first mascot who looks at him funny. The only potential weapons would be the ones security is allowed to have on hand and possibly the knives and other supplies found in the many restaurant kitchens.

The boy cries out to his mother, his nails trying to grip the sun-warmed pavement as he is dragged farther from safety.

There is no more time to think. As one of the slightly higher flying rugs passes by, Ray stupidly reaches out and grabs the safety bar of the ride, pulling himself up to hitch a ride.

Holding tightly to the floor of the open-doored car, Ray brings his knees into his chest, with the soles of his boots flat out in front of him as he lies on his back. He's only got one shot at this. He takes in a breath, and as the car circles by the undead child, Ray swiftly thrusts his legs out, knocking the undead child off.

As soon as he lands the kick, Ray jumps from the car, immediately ducking as the flying rugs continue to fly overhead. Dashing out from under the ride, Ray picks up the young boy and cradles him safely in his arms.

"It's okay. You're going to be okay!" Ray says in a soft yet hurried voice, trying to let the young boy know he is there to help.

This is where Ray will pass the boy off to his mother. They will share a moment of joy as they are reunited, and he will be on his way, but he isn't in the clear yet. No. Between him and the young boy's mother is still the undead child. Plus, this is just one woman. There is no way she will be able to make a getaway to somewhere safe on her own, with two children in tow.

Pissed off, the undead child slowly picked itself up off the ground. His bloodshot eyes wild and wide. His mouth salivating more than a usual human as he exposes his teeth.

Ray holds the frightened boy close in his arms, doing his

best to keep him calm as he feels the boy quiver.

Time to assess the area.

At the ride's entrance, two undead adults are close to figuring out how to get through the queue. At the exit, the mother. Between them, the undead child preparing to strike. Inside Ray's head? Several different scenarios and how each can potentially go wrong.

Time is ticking, and he has to make a choice.

Looking around as quickly as possible, he notes a souvenir shop. The Desert Baroness shop. A golden yellow stone shop with a large, round, red wooden door that is conveniently left partially open. It looks like everyone has already evacuated.

"There," he chokes out, still holding the child. "Meet me inside the shop," he says, praying to God that this woman will trust him.

* * *

The mother looks behind to where Ray is pointing, her stomach twisting at the idea of leaving her son in the hands of a stranger. She doesn't know this guy, but what other choice is there? After all, he did just risk his life to save her son.

With a silent nod, the woman takes a couple of steps back toward the gate. Careful not to startle the undead boy, she gently lifts the little lock on the exit gate, pulling it open and backing out. While she has managed to not alert the undead boy, her movements do not go unnoticed.

"Mommy! Don't go!" her son screams out, not wanting to be left along with this stranger.

"It's okay, Joshua! Hold on tight to that man and don't let go!" she replies with a trembling voice. "Mommy and Aiden will be waiting inside that building! Everything is going to be okay!" she continues as she points toward their meeting spot. Her stomach tightening even more, but as the undead child runs at Ray and Josh, the mother takes off toward the safety of the souvenir shop with her other son.

* * *

"Joshua? A strong name!" Ray says, holding the boy close. "I need you to be strong for me. Think you can do that?"

Josh gives a small nod as he buries his face into Ray's shoulder, his tears soaking into Ray's shirt sleeve.

With a loud hiss, the undead child leaps at Ray, his arms reaching out as he tries to go for a strike.

Ray barely dodges the undead child as his fingernails graze Ray's shirt. Ray lets out a sigh of relief as he narrowly makes it past, but, unfortunately, the two adult undead patrons have finally made their way through the queue, blocking his path.

Standing between the three undead patrons, Ray again assesses his options again. The easiest way for him will be to go under the ride, but that will sacrifice his speed and leave both him and Josh in a vulnerable position.

"Think," Ray mutters to himself, knowing time is of the essence. "Think."

Whoosh. Whoosh. Whoosh.

Ray can feel the breeze of each passing rug on the back of his neck.

Whoosh. Whoosh. Whoosh.

And there it is. The hypothetical lightbulb over Ray's head finally turns on.

"You're going for a ride!" Ray exclaims, turning his back to the undead and hoisting Joshua up and into one of the ride's cars as it passes by. Of course, as he pretty much throws Joshua into the car, the three undead patrons move in, each ready for a strike.

"Oh shit!" Ray mutters to himself, as he has to act quickly.

The three of them all reach out to grab Ray, each with the hopes of sinking their teeth into his raw flesh and ripping him limb from limb to satisfy their never-ending hunger. However, as another rug flies by, Ray reaches up and hitches another ride, this time fully pulling himself onto the car.

As he does this, the undead child runs under the ride, trying to chase from below. But as fast as the undead child is, the ride is faster. With one swoop from a low-flying rug, the undead child's head is taken clean off, and his already dead body falls flat to the ground, his head landing just at the feet of the undead adults.

Chapter 6

Barely able to hold his balance atop one of the moving rug cars, Ray eyes the other cars as he tries to locate Joshua, whom he has recklessly thrown onto the ride without much warning. Probably scaring the child from mundane rides like this for the rest of his life. There Josh is, two cars behind him.

Ray cautiously crouches down as he steps toward the back of the car, preparing to do one of the stupidest things he has ever done in his life.

"You can do this," he mutters to himself as he springs himself off the flying rug into the air. His heart pounds as the flying rug ride continues moving, and all he can see below are the two undead adults, like a couple of hungry sharks waiting for their prey.

As quick as one car disappears, the other appears right on time. Ray makes his landing with a loud *thud* from his shoes. A premature *Oh my God, I fucking did it!* victory yell in his head is followed by an out loud "Oh shit!" as he loses his balance, slipping flat on his stomach.

Ray stretches his arms out to the point of near dislocation to grip the ledge where the passengers sit and the front of the car begins. Dangling off the side of the ride, he practically teases the undead below, as he is in their reach one second, then out of reach the next as the ride continues its circular motion.

With one hand holding onto the ledge, and the other thankfully having a somewhat decent grip as his palm sticks to the metal car, Ray gently pulls himself up. He takes in a deep breath as the muscles in his arms and chest do all the work in pulling him up to safety.

Back in the car, Ray takes a deep breath in. Part of him wonders if he and Josh can just survive on this ride till help comes. But who knows how long that will be? There is no way he can deal with riding this for hours on end. Knowing this, Ray forces himself back up to repeat the stunt he has just pulled, only with more success. He hopes.

"I'm coming. Just stay where you are," Ray calls out to Josh as he assumes the same jumping position as before— knees bent in close to his chest, hands firmly gripping the edge of the ride, and eyes focused on the car behind him.

Ray's adrenalin reaches its peak as his eyes lock on little Joshua. The boy is probably already terrified by the situation, so there is no room for error.

With a quick breath out, Ray launches himself forward toward Joshua on the flying rug behind him. Just like before, as Ray becomes airborne, he watches as the current flying rug disappears beneath his feet and the new flying rug approaches below him. And just like before, he lands firmly lands on the car with a loud *thud*.

Rather than trying to stable himself on the car like before, Ray pushed himself forward one final time with his feet the moment they contact the ride. Awkwardly, Ray flops forward onto his stomach as he takes a hold of the safety bar and pull himself into the seat face first.

With his heart still pounding outside of his chest, Ray sighs in relief. He has never been so happy to be laying face-first on the floor of some questionable carnival ride.

"Mister, are you alright?" a young, innocent, and slightly confused Joshua asks as he gently taps his fingers against the back of Ray's head.

Feeling the touch of the young boy, Ray groans. "Yeah." Though the reality is the adrenalin is wearing off, and he realizes he has no plan from this point.

If the ride comes to a stop, it will allow him a chance to try to jump down and make a run for it toward the rendezvous point with the mother. However, due to some mechanical errors in the little control panel room—the dead ride attendant leaning over the panel and what appear to be several flashing lights on buttons and some indents on the panel—the ride doesn't seem to be stopping any time soon.

For now, Ray decides it is best to utilize a unique feature of the ride. The flying rug has a lever that allows the rider to go higher and lower. As long as the car itself is high, he and Josh are safe, buying Ray time to come up with a plan. Right now, all he has is the hope that the undead below will get bored and wander away, but with each pass of the ride, it seems less and less likely that such a thing will happen.

Chapter 7

"Hey!" a loud booming and deep voice confidently yells from outside the fence surrounding the Flying Rug ride. The voice belongs to a large-chested, tall, bald, yet handsome dark-skinned man. His muscles are chiselled to perfection.

In his hand he holds a large two-by-four that has clearly already been used as it is currently spattered with blood and has many chips missing from it.

The man hops over the gate with ease, drawing the attention of the larger male undead patron, who immediately turns his focus away from the ride. Mouth open and bloodied teeth exposed, the larger undead patron goes into an unsteady run toward the man. Holding his ground, the stranger raises the board as if it were a baseball bat and positions himself in the perfect swinging stance. He holds a tight grip of the wood, keeping his eyes focused on the undead patron. The moment the undead patron is within reach, the stranger steps forward and unleashes a mighty swing.

The undead patron's head jolts to the side, causing the undead patron to stumble and fall. Naturally, as that happens, the female undead patron gives up on her flying prey and turns her attention to the new guy.

While the undead male goes down, she jumps out from behind with a loud, ear-piercing hiss, her eyes wild and out for blood. She leaps at the man, going in for a tackle; however, with some quick movements, the man readjusts the board, lining it with his torso before thrusting it into her torso while she is in mid-jump.

"Hey! You up there, hurry up and get down from there!" he yells to Ray and Joshua.

Ray gives a firm nod as he reaches for the steel lever, lowering the flying rug to the lowest possible setting.

Slowly, the machine lowers itself enough to safely hover above the ground. Ray slides over, then lifts Joshua into his lap. "I need you to hold on to me tight," he says to the young boy, and has Joshua turn to face him.

With his brave face on and trusting that this man is trying to help, Joshua clings to Rays as tight as he humanly can.

Looking down at the spinning ground, Ray takes in a deep breath before giving himself a small push off the side of the ride. He jumps, immediately stumbling forward as his body adjusts from the constant motion to the still ground below. The weight of the six-year-old boy helps make the transition even more tricky. Thankfully, Ray catches himself on the nearby gate, preventing him from falling and crushing the poor child in the process.

Meanwhile, the stranger is just finishing up with the

undead patrons, not even breaking a sweat as he swings the board around. At his feet, the male patron's head is completely bashed in, an unrecognizable, big, gooey pile of blood, ooze, and brains.

The female, still breathing—or whatever you want to call it—is downed, pinned through the torso by the board. While she screams and struggles, not in pain, but rather, still wildly attempting to rip this man's throat out, the stranger begins twisting the board back and forth. Each turn entangles and crushes the undead patron's insides until she finally drops her arm, dead. For real, this time.

With a huffed breath, the stranger removes the board from the undead's stomach and relaxes it on his shoulder like this is some baseball game and he has just casually hit a home run.

"Daddy!" Joshua calls out once the excitement ends, for the moment.

"Daddy?" Ray replies, letting Josh down, who immediately dashes over to the stranger's side. Joshua tightly hugs his dad's legs, trying his best not to cry or show him he is at all scared.

"It's okay, Joshy. I'm here," the man says, crouching down to his son's level. With the board still held with one hand, the man takes Joshua with his free hand, pulling him into a half hug before fully picking the boy up. "Where are your mother and brother?"

"There," Josh replies sheepishly, pointing toward the souvenir shop.

Awkwardly, Ray approaches, overhearing the question about the location of the boy's mother. Seeing that this is indeed the boy's father, he can only assume that the man is talking about the woman he helped at the beginning of the flying rug nightmare. "I told her to wait for us inside," Ray adds, wanting to assure this man that his wife did not suddenly choose to abandon her child to fend for himself.

Chapter 8

The Desert Baroness store. A strategically well-placed marketing ploy set right at the exit of the Flying Rug ride, just bright enough to catch even the attention of the smallest of eyes.

To the young mother's surprise, everything in the shop seems in place. Aside from the fact that there isn't a soul to be seen inside, no customers or employees, it almost looks untouched. It is a relief to step in from the chaos outside into a place of quiet where she can catch her breath.

Completely positive that the store is empty, the young mother locks the door behind her and sets her son down by one of the stuffed toy stands. "Why don't you pick out something for your brother?" she says, trying to keep a calm head, crouching down low, trying to assure him that everything is going to be alright, even though there is an ever-growing knot in her stomach.

"What about me?" Aiden sheepishly says, wanting

something as well.

"Of course!" she replies, gently placing a hand on his head with a soft smile. "Just try to keep quiet, okay?"

Aiden gives a silent nod as he turns his attention from his mother and immediately begins going through the stuffed animals, pulling them off the shelves, one by one, and dropping them onto the floor as he looks for the perfect plush toy. Something soft and fuzzy with the perfect amount of squish to it.

Normally, Aiden and Joshua would be scolded for such behaviour in a store, but for the moment, the young mother doesn't care. The mess her son can make inside this little shop is minuscule compared to the chaos happening outside. A small pile of stuffed animals tossed on the floor is the least of the woman's concerns.

While Aiden is making his little plush pile, trying to decide which one his brother will want, the woman wanders over to the store window. She feels sick. Lost. Confused. Unsure of what is happening and what she is going to do. Not to mention that at this moment, she is separated from her husband who went on a washroom break, and her other son is in the hands of a stranger who is currently trying to fight off those things.

The woman walks over to the window to see if she can get an update as to what is happening outside. Part of her is angry at herself for running away and leaving her child the way she did. What kind of mother is she? What kind of mother runs away when her child needs her the most?

As she looks out the window, she sees no sight of Joshua or Ray. Her heart pounds hard against her chest as possible scenarios flood through her head. At this point, all she can think is that she has left her son for dead. That the last thing Joshua will ever see is his mother taking his younger (by fourteen minutes) brother to safety while he is left there to be torn apart by those creatures roaming the park.

This same thought plays over and over in her head, to the point that she can't look out the window anymore. Instead, she turns her back to the wall and slides herself down until she is seated on the cool floor below. And as much as she tries to hold it together and be strong, she can't control her eyes from beginning to water.

"What have I done?" she chokes out to herself. "I'm so sorry, Joshua . . ."

"Don't cry!" Aiden then says, interrupting his mother's internal breakdown, holding a plush lemur in her face. He waves the plush toy around, its extra-fluffy tail swaying side to side with each movement.

"And who is that?" the woman questions, already knowing the answer, but needing this moment.

Aiden gives a confused pout as he looks at the lemur and then back to his mother. "Lemmy!" he replies. "The lemur who hangs out with Baron Alan and steals things."

"Right, I remember now," she replies, holding out her arms toward her son.

As most children, Aiden knew the universal signal for "Come here. Mommy needs a hug." The sad eyes, the out-stretched arms, and the forced smile. With the lemur still in hand, Aiden crawls into his mother's lap, giving her a big warm hug, closely followed by a *boop* on the nose with the stuffed toy.

Suddenly, there is a loud knocking on the door.

The woman jumps, startled by the noise.

"Wait here," she says as she breaks from the hug to go investigate the door. Carefully, she approaches, her guard up as she yells through the door. "Who is it?"

"Vanessa?" a familiar voice calls out in response.

Her lips can't help but form a smile as she recognizes the voice. Without any hesitation, she opens the door and reveals not only her husband, but her other child held safely in his arms.

"Tom!" she calls out, surprised and overwhelmed with happiness to see her husband, of all people, walk through. Her guard drops as her tense body finally relaxes with relief.

"You've got Joshua!" Vanessa exclaims as tears of joy stream down her cheeks. Immediately, she takes her son from Tom, embracing him tightly. "Are you hurt? I am so sorry, Joshua! I will never leave you again, I promise!"

Josh happily jumps into his mother's arms.

"I isn't scared! I get to ride the flying rugs!" he exclaims as he returns the tight embrace. "Then Daddy came and beat up those bad people!"

While Vanessa is having her family reunion, Ray enters the store, closing the door behind him, relieved that he can finally take a break and process what is even happening.

Chapter 9

A week ago, everything was normal at the Harris residence.

A week ago, everything was perfect.

It is Tom's turn to pick the boys up from pre-school.

It is also Aiden and Joshua's sixth birthday, and this is the year Vanessa and Tom have decided to give the boys a birthday gift they will remember for a lifetime, knowing that they will finally be old enough to create memories unlike anything before.

While Tom is out to get the boys, Vanessa races around the house, trying to make sure everything is perfect.

In the living room, on their low coffee table, are two colourful wrapped boxes. A purple box with "Aiden" written on the tag and a red box with "Joshua" written on the tag.

It is a pretty minimalistic approach to the surprise at hand, but one that Vanessa is sure to be effective. One that is sure to bring out an array of emotions, the main goal being an overwhelming excitement.

Yep.

Everything is perfect and the boys are in for the surprise of a lifetime, alright!

* * *

A car pulls into the driveway. The boys have finally returned.

Vanessa opens it and immediately crouches down to greet her children who, with no hesitation, run into her with loving hugs.

"Did you have a good day at school?" she asks as she receives a big warm hug from Aiden, followed by one from Joshua.

"We made a volcano!" Joshua says in an amazed voice, as if seeing vinegar and baking soda mixed together explode is the coolest thing in his life.

She chuckles as she scoots her boys inside. Standing herself back up, Vanessa watches as Tom struggles to make his way from their van with pizza in one hand and a large brown bag in the other.

"I thought you were just going to get a pizza," she says, acknowledging the added brown bag, now sitting on top of the pizza box.

Tom approaches Vanessa with a smirk on his face as he leans in to greet his gorgeous wife with a kiss. "You try telling Aiden 'No' when he says he'd rather have nuggets instead of pizza for his birthday dinner," he immediately adds, pulling back from Vanessa, twirling himself around her like he is in some sort of pizza commercial.

With a slight roll of her eyes, Vanessa closes the front door.

* * *

All you have to do is go on the internet and look up "Skippy World surprise videos" and hundreds of items will pop up. So many variations of the same concept. Parents telling their children they forgot their birthday, parents hiring a *Vindicator* to show up at the house and present the special message. The things parents do to surprise their children are amazing. And while the approaches to the surprise all vary, the reactions are generally the same.

Children of all ages, unable to contain their excitement. Except for one child who went viral for pretty much being the only child to start crying and claiming she didn't want to go to Skippy World. It was probably staged.

"Now, Daddy and I decided to keep this year small," Vanessa says as she pulls out her cell phone, a move that every parent who follows through with this surprise does. "We think you boys are getting too old for toys."

Holding her phone steady, she places a box beside Aiden (who can care less about what's in the box because he has his nuggets) and the other beside Joshua, who has set his down pizza down beside him. Confusion is showing.

Lifting the box, the paper crinkling beneath his fingers as Joshua gives it a shake. "But I like toys . . ." he says, unsure if he even wants to open the box at this point, seeing that his mom has just confirmed there are no toys inside it.

The box itself isn't very heavy, but there is something inside, as there is a little movement inside.

"You'll like what's inside," Vanessa replies with a snicker. She doesn't even mind that Aiden isn't paying attention to the box because she knows without a doubt that once

Joshua opens his, Aiden's attention will immediately switch over to the box.

"Go get the cake. Kitchen table, white box," Vanessa sneakily whispers to Tom.

Like a good husband, Tom leaves the room to retrieve the special cake that Vanessa has ordered for the boys.

Joshua gives the box another shake.

"Joshy, it's not going to bite you," Tom says, returning to the living room with the cake box in hand. "Aiden, don't you want to open your gift?"

Aiden has just finished shoving his last chicken nugget in his mouth when his dad speaks to him. He gives a shrug as he takes the box in his hand. Unlike his brother, Aiden doesn't care what is in the box.

While Josh contemplates opening the gift, Aiden rips into the paper piece by piece until a brown box is revealed. Aiden then reaches his hands into the box, pulling open the flaps, peering inside to look.

Inside the box: pair of Skippy Squirrel ears. Unlike the standard ears, though, these are coloured and themed as Aiden's favourite Vindicator, Patriotic Commander. The leader of the *Vindicators*, who proudly wears his country's colours: red, white, and blue.

Aiden's eyes lit up. "Oh my gosh! Patriotic Commander!" he excitedly yells.

It doesn't take long for Joshua to clue in as to what is happening. As Aiden pulls out his ears, Joshua savagely rips into his box like a hungry animal trying to scavenge for food.

"Metal Man!" he yells out, wildly pulling out his own ears, immediately tossing the box to the side. These silver and purple, made to look almost metallic.

"A-are we going—?" Joshua starts, unable to get words out as the excitement continues to build inside him.

While Vanessa is grinning behind the camera, recording this golden reaction from her boys, she gives a slight nudge with her elbow to Tom, signalling him to unveil the cake.

Tom himself can feel the excitement emanating from his boys. This energy in the room is just infectious. He used to mock these videos on the internet, thinking they were just some dumb play to try to get internet famous, but now he is starting to get it.

"You tell me," he says, opening the cake box revealing a blue-frosted cake, heavily decorated with balloons with a large number six on them, representing the boys' new age.

Around the border of the cake are images of castles and dragons. There are figurines of the Vindicators sitting atop the cake. In the centre, there is a cute icing drawing of Skippy and Shirley Squirrel, holding a banner.

"You're going to Skippy World!" Joshua and Aiden both read slowly, already guessing they are going, but now it is official because the cake is telling them so.

And now for the final reaction Vanessa has been waiting for.

The dramatics.

While Aiden screams and jumps with excitement, Joshua pretends to faint on the floor, also screaming with joy and even starting to tear up, having believed that his parents weren't going to do anything awesome for his birthday.

And with the click of the stop record button, memories of this life-changing moment are forever saved.

Chapter 10

"911, what is your emergency?"

"Skippy World has become a slaughterhouse! My family and I need help. They're fuckin' everywhere . . ."

"Please try to remain calm. We have already sent dispatch out. Are you someplace safe?"

"If you consider locked inside a store safe while ravenous zombies are lurking just outside the door, sure, we're safe."

"Just remain where you are until help arrives."

As Tom speaks, Ray sits listening by himself, over by the cashier's desk. Even though he isn't able to hear the other side of the conversation, it is pretty clear that Tom is getting the fancy version of "we don't know anything, just that we are getting hundreds of phone calls requesting help at Skippy World."

Letting out a small sigh of exhaustion, Ray gently reaches into his own pocket, removing his own phone.

The phone's screen switches from darkness into bright, radiant light as it brings up the home screen. The background, a photo from just last summer of his wife and daughter taking a goofy photo together while playing at the park. It is a photo from a simpler time.

Opening up the gallery, Ray flicks his thumb across the screen. Each swipe bringing up a new photo. First day of school, showing off her missing tooth, Christmas morning, mother/daughter baking time, awkward beach selfies, every memory captured.

"Here."

Having raided the store's mini-fridge, Vanessa approaches, offering Ray a bottle of water.

"Thanks," Ray says quietly, taking the bottle. Usually, these bottles cost about eight dollars, but under the circumstances, they doubt they'll get in trouble for not paying. He unscrews the lid and takes a giant gulp from the water, realizing that he is actually thirstier than he thought. Then again, the situation has finally caught up to him, and the adrenalin has worn off. Things around him just feel dead. This world has collapsed.

Attached to her other hand is Joshua, who is holding a piece of paper out to Ray.

With the help of some printer paper Vanessa has found under the cash and a bunch of pens and markers from inside the drawer, she and the twins are mostly quietly colouring. While Aiden is drawing dinosaurs and other random stuff, Joshua insists on making something for their new friend.

"I made you a picture," Joshua says in a comforting tone.

For a moment, Ray lowers his phone. His worn

expression fades a little into a smile as the young boy holds the paper up. It is the simplest of gestures, but it really touches him that Josh has gone through this effort.

"You didn't have to," Ray replies politely, taking the paper and unfolding it. It is like the drawings his daughter used to make him. Cute little stick figure people (one of them with a superhero cape), a happy sunshine, and a rainbow. Across the top is writing that clearly has help from his mother, that reads, "Thank you for being a 'ray' of light!"

"You drew this? It's so good!" Ray adds, genuinely touched that he has received such a gift. "I am going to keep this forever."

Feeling proud of his drawing and loving the compliment on his artwork, Joshua gives a nice firm nod before letting go of his mother's hand so that he can return to Aiden's side to draw another picture.

Ray folds the picture up, placing it in his breast shirt pocket for safekeeping.

"I really am grateful you showed up when you did," Vanessa says softly as she glances down, noticing the pictures on Ray's phone, currently a selfie of Ray and Bella posing with their boarding passes.

"Is that your daughter?" she then adds, taking a seat beside Ray.

Silently, Ray gives a nod. "Bella," he replies, as he skips to the next photo, Bella claiming her bed in the hotel room.

"Her mother passed a little over a month ago, so I thought maybe a daddy/daughter trip would take her mind off of things. After all, this is 'the most joyful place in the universe,'" he states with a small chuckle that lasts about two seconds with a forced smile.

The final photo, taken moments before her encounter with Baroness Emberella. An innocent girl with such life in her eyes. A bright smile that can light up any room. To Ray, Bella is one of the strongest people he knows. Despite her young age, she is so brave. Never afraid to face whatever challenges come her way.

With another swipe, a video pops up.

"You're next! You excited!" Ray's voice says in the video, as it focuses in on Bella.

"Yes! I can't believe it! I'm so excited! This is so amazing!" Bella squeals with excitement.

What Ray wanted to capture was this magical interaction between his daughter and Emberella. What Ray has actually captured is her final moments.

Realizing what is about to come next in the video, Ray frantically turns off his phone, immediately pocketing it.

Vanessa knows right away not to press further about his daughter. Even without seeing the footage, Ray's body language is easy to read. He is quiet and while on the outside, he tries to keep himself calm, it is clear that he is in a lot of pain on the inside.

Not wanting to make things awkward, Vanessa glances over to her husband, who is clearly getting annoyed with how dispatch seems to not be taking the situation seriously.

Chapter 11

Tom has just finished on the phone with the police. Unfortunately, they aren't the best of help. All he is told is to seek shelter and remain hidden till the authorities get to the scene.

Sure, sitting still would be fine, if it weren't for the ever-growing number of those undead patrons outside, waiting for someone to naively wander out into the open unprotected.

"That is a complete waste of t——" Tom says with frustration before being cut off by blood-curdling screams coming from outside, closely followed by the sounds of low moans and growls.

Tom cringes at the sounds, his blood boiling at how lightly this situation is being taken. "That is it. We are getting out of here," he states, getting restless.

Sitting on the cashier's counter is a little stand that holds dozens of little park maps and fliers.

Tom takes one of the park maps, unfolds it, and places it firmly on the counter.

The park map, though small when folded, stretches out to be about the standard size of a road map because this is no ordinary amusement park. See, Skippy World is comprised of four full-sized amusement parks, each with their own themes.

Whimsical Dominion, Creature Domain, COPET, and Cinema Gallery.

Obviously, they are in Whimsical Dominion.

With a marker in hand, Tom scribbles a circle over the shop they are currently inside and an X over the main entrance to the park, as it is obviously out of the question.

"Assuming everyone flooded the main gates in their mass panic, the back entry should be our best bet," Tom says, circling the other side of Whimsical Dominion. "Here we have the back entry parking lot, the monorail station, and the ferry to the jungles of Creature Domain. If we can't leave this park, we make it out through Creature Domain."

"Great idea! Let's all head out into the zombie-infested park. Unarmed," Ray replies, chiming in with his thoughts, finally pulling himself off the floor and back to reality.

Kock. Knock. Knock.

Just outside the door, a frantic voice calls out.

"Open the door!" the voice says.

"Please!" another voice calls out in the same panic. "Please, for the love of God, help!"

Ray, Tom, and Vanessa all jump, startled by the unexpected knocking. The three of them give each other the same looks, knowing that letting these strangers inside could put their own lives at risk. At the same time, if it were any of them at the door, crying for refuge during a time like this, they would pray that the people inside would show mercy.

Biting her lip, Vanessa makes the first move by checking out the window to see who is outside. Following her lead, Tom picks up his wooden board and approaches the door with Ray. Both of them wait for Vanessa to give them the all-clear.

Outside, a frightened teenage couple.

"Let them in," Vanessa states to her husband, noting they are currently alone.

As she speaks, Ray quickly opens the door as Tom herds the couple inside the safety of the shop. Before returning himself, he takes a quick scan of the outside, looking to see if there is anyone else nearby who needs help.

"Jesus fuck," Tom mutters quietly.

Body parts lie scattered around the park's ground, blood splattered everywhere. Only a couple hours have passed and this magical place has already become a living hell.

While a group of undead patrons are fascinated by the Flying Rugs ride, which is still moving, a few more are wandering away from the main entrance pathway, spreading themselves throughout the main park, as most of the people who had bottlenecked the way out were either lucky enough to get out, are dead, or are now one of just one of those things.

Just across from the shop are three teenage kids, each armed with some sort of blunt object. One holds a fire extinguisher, another what appears to be a frying pan, and the last one holds a board with a bunch of knives heavily duct-taped to the end.

With the board held high, the teen lets out a war cry before charging toward some undead patrons. He firmly brings it down, sinking a duct-taped knife into its shoulder. However, as he goes to pull it out, the tape snaps, releasing that knife and allowing the other attached to come loose like a cheap toy.

Shocked that his flimsy modification failed, the teen drops the board and turns to run. Unfortunately, his demise is quick, as he himself is not. As for his friends, they *bravely* drop their makeshift weapons, abandoning their friend as they make their getaway.

On the roof of the building behind them, three more teenagers are stuffing pieces of cloth into glass bottles of alcohol raided from one of the park's restaurants. A fourth teen, the oldest-looking of the group, stands near the edge of the roof, leaning over slightly as he observes the kid below getting devoured.

The oldest teenager stretches out his hand toward the three behind him and within a second, a glass bottle is placed in his hand. With the bottle held firmly in his left hand, the teenager takes out a lighter with his right hand. With a few flicks of the lighter, a flame is ignited and the cloth is set aflame. With a crazed grin on his face, the teenager hurls it at the undead patron below.

As the bottle breaks, the undead patron bursts into flames, causing the patron to go into a small frenzy before the fire fully consumes its body, bringing it down until all that is left is a burned corpse. The scent of burning flesh fills the air.

The scene itself is horrific, but in a twisted way, those teenagers look as if they are enjoying this all too much.

To each their own.

Tom steps back inside, pulling the door closed behind him.

Chapter 12

"Thank you," the girlfriend says between breaths as she and her boyfriend stumble into the stop.

"No one else will open up," the boyfriend adds with an exhausted sigh. Their dirtied, torn clothes and sweaty yet sunburned skin indicate that they have been outside for quite some time. "We've had a couple close calls," the boyfriend casually states seconds before collapsing into his partner's arms.

The girlfriend catches him, confused by this sudden change in health. "Babe?" she asks, gently lowering herself and her partner onto their knees. "He's probably just dehydrated; can you get him some water?"

"Yeah, sure," Vanessa replies.

The boyfriend's breaths become irregular as he struggles to grasp for air. His complexion fades to a lifeless grey as he burrows his head into his girlfriend's shoulder.

Returning with a bottle, Vanessa notices a small rip in

the boyfriend's shirt just below his shoulder blade that is soaked blood from a few small lacerations the couple clearly failed to mention.

"How did he get that wound on his back?" Vanessa asks suspiciously as she drops the water bottle, pulling her children in close to her, each taking a hold of a leg.

The girlfriend is genuinely confused. The pair has been chased a couple times, but she doesn't recall any physical altercations, at least that she is aware of. However, as she slides her right hand down his back, she feels it. The warm sticky goo oozing out of what she can only assume is a couple of lacerations from an animal or an undead person trying to rip her boyfriend's face off.

"No," the girlfriend says in denial. "It's not what you think it is!"

Vanessa steps back with her children while her husband grips his weapon tightly.

"You should get away from him," Ray says, cautiously approaching, offering a helping hand toward the girl. "Now."

As Ray speaks, the young woman grasps her partner tighter. "No, he's fine!" she exclaims, refusing to leave his side. "It-it's probably from one of the wire fences we crawled under or something!" she continues, trying to rationalize where the back wound came from.

Shooting a glare at the room, the woman refuses to move from her spot. Her partner inhales loudly, as if he is taking in a large breath of air after being submerged in water for a long period. He then lifts his arms and returns the embrace to the young woman, his head still resting on his shoulder.

"Babe!" she says, letting out a relieved breath. "I am so—"

Holding her tightly, the boyfriend digs his fingernails deep into the woman's back. His nails penetrate her shirt and then her skin.

The girl screams in pain as her now-undead partner digs his fingers into her flesh. While his fingers are still in her back, he rips them out, tearing her skin as he pulls his hands across her back and out the sides, leaving long scratches across her back that look like she has been mauled by a savage tiger. As his hands go free into the air, his mouth opens wide.

The girl screams.

With one swift motion, the undead boyfriend leans in, as if going for a passionate kiss. Only his intentions are not those of romance, catching her upper lip with his teeth. The girlfriend's screams become muffled. Blood fills her mouth, some of it dripping out of the corners, the rest filling her mouth and travelling through her throat into her lungs, causing her to drown in the warm red liquid.

As this scene unfolds before them, Vanessa immediately picks up Aiden in one arm and Joshua in her other.

This sudden movement catches the undead boyfriend's attention. He pulls himself up, ripping the girl's lip across her cheek like a BAND-AID before letting go and turning his attention to Vanessa. His eyes roll back into his head, blood dripping from his mouth. The undead boyfriend lets out a hiss.

"Fuck this! We need to go!" Tom exclaims.

As the undead boyfriend is about to make a move, his head is met with the large board that has been collected by Tom. The undead boyfriend is knocked onto the ground, stunned for just a moment.

"Looks like we're going with your plan," Ray says, noting that the woman just murdered by her partner has just reopened her eyes.

Of course, when Tom had the idea of making a run for it, he wasn't meaning this exact moment. They needed to figure out the safest route, arm themselves, and move stealthily. The plan was not to just run out into the open like this.

With no other choice and knowing that even if they kill these two so that they actually stay down, there is no way he is having his kids in the same room. This whole situation is already adding up to years of therapy. Last thing he wants on the list is how Mommy and Daddy kept them hunkered in a room with two rotting corpses while waiting for help.

Quickly, Ray throws open the door, running out first to ensure it is clear before signalling Vanessa to follow behind.

"Come on!" Ray calls out to Tom, who is ensuring his family gets out safely.

Hearing his name, Tom swings the board one final time at the undead boyfriend, quickly backing out of the store. Just in time, too, because as they close the door, the woman is just getting back up off the ground.

Both Ray and Tom lean up against the door, holding it closed as the undead girlfriend wails, slamming herself into the door, and scratching intensely at it, determined to get out.

Chapter 13

The raging undead on the inside have finally given up on trying to break out of the shop. Tom cautiously peers through the window to take a peek inside before turning to Ray with a thumbs up, confirming that they have moved away from the door. Ray takes in a deep breath of relief as his racing heart finally returns to a slower pace. That was too close for comfort.

However, the moment is as cheery music plays throughout the park.

The music starts off light and whimsical, with ocarinas, flutes, and harps harmonizing together to create a mellow melody. After a few seconds, the music's volume lowers as it takes a back seat to an over-the-top voice.

"Greetings, my squirrelly cadets! It's me! Skippy!"

"And Shirley!" a second, more feminine voice says.

"And we'd like to invite you to our spectacular parade of wonders!" they both say in unison.

The voices each cut out, and the music becomes more energetic as trumpets boom through the speakers. The noise lures undead patrons from across the park as if they are rats following the hypnotic sounds of the pied piper's flute.

Suddenly, a glass bottle shatters inches from Tom's foot. As it hits the ground, it releases the liquid inside and immediately ignites. Luckily, with his quick reflexes, Tom leaps to the side, avoiding catching fire.

"Hey! Watch it!" he furiously yells, noticing it has come from the teens hiding up on the roof of the Desert Diner. All of them are now gathered atop the roof, mostly hanging out and eager to kill some zombies like they do in their video games.

"My bad!" the tallest teen replies, having mistaken Tom and the others as undead patrons. "But you might want to start running."

"Shit," both Tom and Ray say practically in unison.

As the music continues to play, a parade of undead gets closer and closer.

Approaching in this crowd are undead patrons of all ages. There is a woman with her jaw just barely hanging onto her face with one strand of skin, eyes wild and lifeless. Beside her, a young boy, missing his left ear, with his chest ripped open.

Numerous maimed park employees are also mixed into the crowd, their once-perfect uniforms completely shredded and soaked in blood. Their once-friendly faces replaced with expressions of rage and hunger.

There is even Skippy's best friend, Gary Goose. No, it isn't actually a goose (which is more terrifying), but a poor worker in an oversized mascot costume. Unfortunately, it seems even the thick foam is not protection enough, as there is a gaping hole torn out of the mascot's left torso. The feathers around the hole are just completely stained red, while his large intestine hangs out the side like a chain from a wallet.

It is just an endless parade of death and despair.

Taking a note from the teens, Tom decides that their next best bet will be to get the higher ground. From what he can tell, these things do not have the capability to climb. Or at least that is his thought process behind it. He honestly has no idea what these things can do.

Without a word and with only one direction to travel (away from the parade of undead), Tom, Ray, and Vanessa take off, running down the park's streets, the desert theme of the buildings transitioning into something from out of old France.

While the three of them frantically search for a way onto the building's roof, the overly excited and unsupervised teenagers on the desert diner roof begin lighting the cloth ends of their Molotov cocktails, hurling them at the large crowd of undead, instantly igniting them.

The teens all cheer with excitement.

One bottle even hits Gary Goose, completely engulfing him in flames. While most people would be screaming in pain as they burned to death, the fire only makes the goose more aggressive.

With his feathers aflame and his intestines unravelling behind him, he charges toward the building, reaching up to try to get to the kids. Several others follow suit, all scratching away at the bricks in attempts to climb up.

"Over here!" Ray calls out, spotting a couple barrels and crates just beside Garson's Pub. Ray stands to the side, gesturing for Vanessa to go ahead of him, the priority being to get her and her kids to safety.

Holding onto her boys tightly, Vanessa dashes toward Ray. However, as she passes the pub, the doors swing open, and a crazed Garson comes stumbling out, his jugular completely torn out. His usual chiselled jaw is dislocated and locked to the left side of his face. He jumps out at Vanessa and the twins.

"Shit!" Vanessa exclaims as she has barely any time to react.

Thankfully, it is husband Tom to the rescue. Still with his board in hand. Tom charges at the undead Garson, holding the board straight out in front. With the impact of the board, Garson is pushed away from Vanessa and knocked to the ground. The board snaps, the end breaking off, leaving sharp, splintered edges.

Suddenly, three more undead come running their way.

"Go, I'll be right behind you!" Tom huffs out, holding the broken board up, still ready to fight to protect his family.

With her boys in hand, Vanessa knows she has to get them to safety. "You better be!" she states firmly, getting the boys to Ray.

Having already climbed up onto the pub's roof, Ray reaches down over the ledge. With no hesitation, Vanessa first passes Joshua to him and then Aiden.

"Now you!" Ray says, extending his hand out to help Vanessa up. Only, by the time he has leaned back over the edge, she is gone. He looks around the little alley, and then out to where Tom is, confused as to where she has disappeared to in such a short time.

Tom is obviously getting worn out. He is a big guy, incredibly healthy, loves sports. Works out every day and never has smoked, but everyone has their limits, even the most active of people. Right now, it just seems like every time he takes out a ravaging undead patron, two, sometimes three more appear. With his board whittling down to what is essentially a twig, Tom is realizing that this is going to be it. But at least he is going to go out fighting.

Chapter 14

I t doesn't take long for the flames from the Gary Goose costume to light up the Desert Diner, where the group of teenagers currently resides.

The once-funny-looking bird, dressed as a pilot, now consumed by the flames. The eyes of the costume, slowly melting away into rubber tears, revealing the poor employee beneath. His face unrecognizable from both the horrific transformation he has endured and the flesh bubbling from the heat of the flames.

As the flames get higher and begin spreading throughout the building, the teens realize it is time for them to move on; it is only a matter of time before the flames will engulf the entire building.

The tallest of the group, a young male by the name of Tyler, who has to be about seventeen years old, is visiting the park with his girlfriend, Michelle, for their three-month anniversary.

Both of them avid gamers who live for ultraviolence. While it is a fluke that they are in the park on this day, as soon as the chaos breaks out, the pair implements what the games taught them in real life.

While people are running away, the couple collect supplies. As this park has a no weapons policy, and guns and ammo won't just be lying around like in those games, they have to get a little creative, and creative they get. Hitting up the various shops and restaurants, they quickly fill their backpacks up with bottles of alcohol, random shirts, lighters, knives, and whatever they think might be helpful.

Even in the short couple of hours, they have recruited a few others to their fight. Kids who have lost their parents and are trying to run for their lives or other teenagers who feel they are ready to take on a zombie apocalypse. Though Tyler has some criteria, he has to be the one in charge, which is why he doesn't end up recruiting anyone older than him. There is no chance in hell he will allow anyone to give him orders.

Quickly, Michelle packs the remaining Molotov cocktails into her backpack.

"Come on!" Tyler calls out as he dashes to the building beside the diner, leaping between the buildings, landing with a small roll before catching himself.

Right behind him, a boy around the age of sixteen follows suit, jumping without hesitation and landing on the roof rather roughly as it really isn't a small jump and he is not physically prepared for this, but being young, energetic, and feeling the rush of the moment helps.

One by one, the teenagers leap from the burning

building to the roof of the shop next door, trying to keep the high ground so that they can have more of an advantage against the undead patrons.

"Hey! Wait up!" Michelle calls out to Tyler, just having to get everything stuffed in her bag and scrambling to get herself up. She quickly picks herself up and takes off running toward the end of the flaming building, only to stop at the edge, completely hesitant to make the jump to the other side, realizing the gap from her building to theirs is quite wide. Biting her lip, Michelle looks down. Though the fall itself isn't too high, and she will most likely walk away with minimal damage, she will be cornered. If she doesn't make this jump, she will be fucked.

"Seriously?" Tyler mutters to himself, looking back at his girlfriend. His expression changes to unimpressed at how his girlfriend is apparently afraid to jump.

"Just come on!" he yells unsympathetically, with haste and annoyance.

His yell draws the attention of the undead patrons. Slowly, they stumble over each other, making their way toward the building next door, eyes still on the kids above.

Rolling his eyes, Tyler lets out an annoyed breath and reaches over the ledge, arm extended. "I'll catch you," he says with frustration. "Throw the bag over first."

It makes sense; the bag is heavy. So, without question, she tosses the bag to Tyler. Tyler catches the bag with his right hand, then drops it beside him on the roof so he can turn his attention back to Michelle. "Okay, now you!" he says, reaching his arms back out again toward the other building where Michelle stands.

Michelle gives a nod and takes a few steps backwards. She takes a deep breath in and runs. With one swift motion, she leaps off the edge of the building toward the one beside. She reaches out her hands; however, just as she is about to be caught by Tyler, he raises his hand away.

Caught off guard, Michelle crashes into the side of the building, just barely catching herself on the roof, her hands slipping against the brick. "What are you doing? Help me up!" she cries out, struggling to pull herself up as she dangles over the side, her upper body strength really not that great. It is almost like that scene from *Big Cat Monarch*, where Ataturk is hanging off a mountain and his brother, Flaw, watched as Ataturk fell to his demise at the bottom of the mountain, where a herd of stampeding elephants were waiting.

"You're just going to slow me down," Tyler states flatly, taking her backpack and slinging it over his shoulder. She may be his girlfriend, but that doesn't mean he likes her. In actuality, their relationship was never great to begin with. Michelle isn't good at games, often causing Tyler to die, thereby "ruining his online reputation." Seeing Michelle struggling to pull herself up reminds him of all the times he is downed in-game and she can't figure out which button to use to revive him. Their relationship is incredibly toxic and has been failing since the day they met. To Tyler, this is the perfect way to just end it.

In this situation, Tyler feels that if any of these brats are going to get in his way, slow him down, or go against his word, he has no issues dropping them. If zombie games taught Tyler anything, it is that you only care for yourself, and, well, always go for the headshot. Luckily, none of the other kids he has recruited are close by to see what he is doing, as they have all continued ahead to meet at the rendezvous.

Within moments, the undead horde below takes hold of Michelle's legs. She lets out a loud scream as she holds on for dear life, kicking to try to get them away as her lower torso is slowly stretched as the hands of many start clawing and pulling at her legs.

Unable to hold on anymore, her hands slip from the roof, her nails scraping hard against the brick walls, breaking off and leaving a trail of blood as she's pulled to the ground. Her screamer s quickly silenced as her body is being ripped apart, limb from limb.

Chapter 15

A nother undead patron falls, readying to get up before its head suddenly bursts into a massive bloody mess, repeatedly smashed in by Tom and the remaining piece of wood. Each hit makes the undead patron more and more unrecognizable to the human eye.

While Tom is distracted by smashing in its head, an undead baroness jumps on him from the back, forcing the larger man onto the ground.

Baroness Chime, the woman of Garson's dreams. One of Vanessa's favourites because she is a simple baroness who enjoys the little things in life and finds the beauty in the most heinous of creatures. Usually shown with her hair tied up into a French braid, while wearing a light green sundress with a book in hand, this infected beauty is missing half her skull. Her hair is frayed and tangled, while her right eye is barely hanging on by the optic nerve as it dangles down her cheek. The simple green dress is just completely ripped and torn, spattered with blood and dirt.

Tom gets her off momentarily, only to have her make her way back on top as he rolls himself over. Quickly, he stretches out his arms into the air, raising his board up like a small barrier between him and the baroness. As the board pushes Chime slightly away, her head droops down and hovers just above Toms. Her teeth snap at him as her loose eye sways like a pendulum just inches from his face.

Now, the only thing between him and Baroness Chime is a blood-stained piece of wood he found by the washrooms back when he and his wife got separated.

With his arms giving out, the board being held up slowly eases in close to Tom's face. The deranged Chime, growling and snapping her jaw like a rabid dog, gets closer and closer.

Tom closes his eyes tightly as he prepares for the end. Only, as he does so, the weight atop of him disappears. He reopens his eyes, just in time to see Chime's head separate from her body. The skin from her neck rips as it falls off to the ground beside him. As her head is severed, her body goes completely limp, lying lifeless on top of Tom, who is positive this is the end.

Standing just above Tom, hand extended out to help him up with a bloodied axe in her hand, is his soul mate. The woman he married, Vanessa.

Without question, he takes Vanessa's hand. He stands himself up, tossing the lifeless body of Chime to the side. He takes a moment to catch his breath and dust himself off (while checking for any open wounds) before looking back at his wife with an arched brow.

"Where did you find that?" are the first words from his mouth.

"The pub," she states with a small shrug.

* * *

When she passes her children up to Ray, Vanessa notices the fire emergency station just through the bar's window. Most importantly, the axe. It is at that moment Vanessa knows what she has to do.

The inside of the building just reeks of blood and death. Then again, there are bodies everywhere. It is just the scene of a massacre. Most likely people who were trying to get to safety but could not escape the fast-spreading plague of the undead.

Entering it just makes Vanessa feel completely sick to her stomach, but she has two young boys she is not raising alone. Her husband's last words to her are not going to be a broken promise.

Chapter 16

Slinging Michelle's backpack over his shoulder, atop his own bag, Tyler jumps off the roof of a building far away from the fires, toward the entrance line of the park's most popular ride, Water's Bluff. Your basic log ride, only it takes the rider through the mountain while puppets tell stories, distracting you from the inevitable plunge down the mountainside.

To Tyler, it is the perfect place to hide out, as most people will be hunkering down in restaurants and shops. Even if there are creepy ass puppets throughout the ride that like to sing, they only go off when a rider comes through on a log. And with his camp set up near the ride's peak, there are only two ways for anyone to reach them. Either through the back maintenance door that staff use or by hitching a ride and hopping off before the log disappears over the edge.

Tyler hurries through the ride's line-up, hopping over the railing like a natural line jumper, free to do as he wants.

The line—which starts outside by a sign stating "the wait time is two hours from this point"—twists into a man-built cave. Upon entry into the cave, patrons are greeted by nonsensical upbeat music and a repetitive voice explaining some story behind the ride along with the do's and don't of Bluff Mountain.

Making his way into the ride's cave, reaching the docking station, Tyler throws his bags into a log and crosses over to the other side of the platform where the control panel is set up. With the setup being made to be run by teenagers, it really is easy for him to know how to kick-start the next log in line to move. Then again, it would take a moron not to see the large green button with "Go" written on it.

Tyler slams his hand down on the button, and fake smoke exhausts from the log setting sail. Dashing from the control panel, Tyler hops into the seat of the log as the annoying voice speaks.

"Hey there, squirrel cadets! Welcome to Water's Bluff! Please keep your arms and legs inside the ride and remember to have a splashing good time!"

Puppets lining the walls of the cave begin to awkwardly move, cutting down trees, shaving the bark down, and just working away.

Sounds of buzzing and chopping play as characters chatter among themselves, telling some lame story about how they are helping a bunch of beavers build a dam. Because apparently beavers need help building dams.

* * *

Just to the left of the track, entering the view of the rider just a few feet ahead, five teenagers are hanging out on the platform. A young girl, roughly fifteen, by the name of Katie, is just sitting with her back against the mountain wall with a bag of chips in her hand. The boy from before, Michael, is busy dismantling the moving puppets for his own enjoyment. Adrian, a seventeen-year-old goth girl and her younger brother Steve, who is fifteen, are sitting by a fake mushroom table with a deck of cards in hand as they play games. And then there is Jeremy, a fourteen-year-old redhead who is just innocently polishing a couple of knives.

Scattered around on the floor are piles of drinks and snacks, clearly stolen from the shops below. Everything from chips, cookies, soda, and water, because the only thing the ride water is good for is rinsing blood off.

Scattered across a table once occupied by puppets is a variety of items the teens have collectively gathered that can prove useful in a fight.

Seeing that guns are not an option, if it can hit with blunt force or set things on fire, it is perfect.

* * *

With a quick shift in gears, the log turns vertical. The chain clicks rapidly as it pulls the car up. This is Tyler's stop. Taking the two backpacks in hand, he throws them over the side onto the platform with the puppets, close to where the camp is set up. Tyler then takes a leap himself, abandoning the log as it finishes its ascent to the top of the mountain, reaching its peak and teetering a little over the edge before making its final descent. As the lights dim and the gears stop, the sound of rushing water can be heard from just inside the tunnel. There is suddenly a loud *splash* followed by some much-needed silence, indicating the ride has finished its cycle.

"Where's your girlfriend?" Adrian asks curiously in a low tone as she glances up from her cards, seeing Tyler finish his journey to the top of the cave, noting that the girl he was with when they first met is no longer with him.

"She didn't make it," Tyler replies without any emotion or concern as he drags the bags over to the weapons table to unload loot.

"Sorry to hear that," Adrian says as she places a card down, ending her play against her brother.

"Don't be," Tyler states, slamming the bags down, ending the conversation as he does not want to get into details.

Opening the first backpack, he pulls out a few more bags of chips, tossing them into their little stockpile of food on the floor. Next to come out is a large cleaver, some carving knives, and several bottles of oil, which join the pile on the table.

Item by item, he unloads and sorts the bag's contents until it is completely empty, starting the process all over again with the other bag.

Chapter 17

Most of the streets are cleared of the living and filled with aimlessly wandering undead patrons. Each slowly makes their way up and down the park's streets with no clear direction other than to feed their never-ending hunger for raw flesh.

Ray, Tom, Vanessa, and the twins have moved along the safety of the roofs and allow themselves to get closer to the park's other entrance, which they hope to reach before sundown. With the time closing in on 6:00 p.m., there isn't much time left in the light, and the last thing the group wants is to be out in the open, completely vulnerable.

Having reached the last rooftop in a chain of buildings, the group has two choices.

Stay there and wait for help that is probably not coming.

Quickly make their way just past Bluff Mountain to the docks, continuing with the original plan.

Naturally, not wanting to take their chances, the three

adults unanimously decide that it is best to keep moving, knowing there is a strong chance things outside are turning to shit as well.

"Let me check things out," Ray says calmly, deciding that if anyone is going to survive this, it is going to be Vanessa and her family. He feels there isn't much left for him. Believing that the least he can do is help his new friends to safety.

"Take this," Vanessa says, passing Ray the axe she took from Garson's Pub, not objecting to his decision to take the lead.

Ray hesitantly takes the weapon before easing toward the building's edge and jumping down.

"Careful," both Vanessa and Tom say, knowing it is safer for one person to go down to scope out the scene, rather than everyone at once.

Ray starts with the building he just jumped down from. One made to look like a wooden cabin belonging to the original baroness, Frozen Ivory. The fair-skinned beauty, who sings to animals and moves in with seven little people.

The inside of the cabin shop is a complete disaster. Starting with the obvious, a young woman, an employee to be more specific, is hunched over the cashier's desk. Blood flows from her torn-up face and neck, still wet and dripping down the cash counter into a puddle on the floor.

Shattered glass is scattered along the floor, broken fragments that lie in a mix of water and blood leading toward the base of what used to be a medium-sized snow globe, resting gently in a toddler's hands.

Aside from those two bodies inside, it is safe to say that

the building has been vacated. The assailants have moved on.

Ray moves on a little farther through the park, checking his blind spots every other moment, as one can never be too cautious. As he walks through the empty street, he holds the axe up high and ready in case he needs it.

Aside from a few undead patrons scattered few and far between, everything seems clear. The undead patrons he does see seem a little preoccupied with either getting into another building or enjoying a fresh corpse. If they are going to make a move, this moment of quiet will probably be the best as the attention is currently away from them.

Returning to Vanessa and Tom's view, Ray raises the axe into the air and signals that it's safe for them to come down.

"Let's go," Tom says to Vanessa, acknowledging Ray's signal that all is clear.

* * *

While the adults seem to have their shit together, Aiden and Josh really have no idea what is going on. This is supposed to be the most joyful place in the universe, yet here they are, running, hiding, and being passed between parents as they are constantly being told that everything is going to be okay.

When things get too gruesome, Vanessa is usually there to keep the boys distracted, doing her best to shield them from the horrors around them. When they want to cry, Vanessa (and sometimes Ray) steps in with a lecture about being brave.

The moment everyone is back together on the sidewalk, the boys cling to Vanessa, each taking a hand in theirs as they hold on tightly. Both of them are trying to keep that brave face on.

The five of them keep close to each other as they cautiously walk down the middle of the street toward what they all hope will be a clear way out. On the left is Tom. On the right, Ray, holding his axe up and ready for anything. Between them, Vanessa with her boys on each side, each holding a hand. Both of them are scared and confused as to what is happening around them.

As much as they would like things to just be simple for once, with the current situation, that is near impossible. The group hasn't ventured far from the cabin shop; in fact, they have just passed the first rollercoaster, Quarry Train, and are just about to continue on past Water's Bluff, with the worst possible timing.

Click.

Click.

Click.

Over at the Water's Bluff ride at the top of the mountain, a log emerges from a dark tunnel. Ever so slowly, the front half topples and in the blink of an eye, the whole log down the mountain, water loudly splashing along its sides until it reaches the bottom, creating a tidal wave that echoes across the park.

"We have to get out of here, now," Tom says quickly, knowing that noise has to alert the undead, luring them to their location like a hungry child being summoned to dinner via a ringing bell.

Chapter 18

Right on cue, low moans and footsteps can be heard from behind. Tom, Vanessa, and Ray all stop, turning to see what they are up against.

Hundreds of undead. All trudging along at their own pace, making their way toward the ride. Some of them drag their feet as they walk with a limp, and others crawl on the ground as their bodies have been severed. And right at the front, a familiar young girl.

"Ray?" Vanessa says with concern in her voice.

Ray goes silent as his heart sinks as his eyes lock on the girl. The noise around him fades into a low ringing before eventually turning to complete silence as the world fades to black, with just one thing in focus under a spotlight. Bella. Why does it have to be Bella?

Seeing that Baroness Emberella's castle is near the front of the park, Bella has wandered quite the distance. Though, perhaps it isn't just aimless wandering. Maybe there is a part of Bella still inside? Maybe she has been searching for her dad? Maybe Bella is still in there, somewhere?

More realistically, it is just a fluke and, like all the other undead, she is just looking for a snack.

Ray lowers his axe as Bella walks toward him. His eyes gloss over with tears as he gazes upon his beautiful little girl. Though her skin is grey, her body mangled and covered in blood, all he can see is his special, bright-eyed girl with her thick brown wavy hair. His little baroness with a smile so contagious it is impossible to be upset around her. She is everything a father could wish for and more.

* * *

April 27, 2015, 2:36 a.m., Bella Maria Holland is born, and she is perfect. The spitting image of her mother and the most important thing in the world.

The first year flew by so fast. He can still picture his baby girl sitting in the high chair, completely unaware of what was happening as they placed a cupcake with a single candle before her. She barely even touched the soft chocolate-flavoured treat. Well, she touched it. A lot. But most of it ended up smeared all over her clothes and thrown on the floor, as it was apparently more fun to play with the food than eat it.

Bella's third birthday was when they received the news: Maria had been diagnosed with a rare illness that is untreatable. All they could do was make every moment count.

Her mother was a true fighter, a trait that Bella shared. Not long after Bella's sixth birthday, Maria succumbed to her illness, peacefully passing away in her sleep. While Bella and Ray were both deeply saddened by this loss, they were grateful that they had those extra years with her.

Ray can still see her beside him at Maria's funeral. Bella gripping his hand, trying not to cry because she wanted to show everyone she was strong like her mother. It was the day that Ray taught her that crying didn't make her weak. While tears ran down Ray's face, he told her that no matter what, he would always be by her side.

* * *

"Ray! What are you doing!" Tom harshly yells out, noticing the faceoff between Ray and this particular undead little girl. "We need to go!"

As tears continued to flow down his cheeks, Ray takes in a slow breath. This thing standing before him is no longer his little girl. His little girl died back at the fortress. No. What stands before him is nothing but an empty shell of what used to be.

"Go on ahead. I will be right behind you." Ray replies, knowing he can't leave Belle this way.

Quietly, Ray steps toward Bella. His heart pounds harder and harder with each step. His eyes are completely focused on Bella as tears blur his focus. Flashes of his daughter form overtop her undead self as his heart feels as though it is ripping in half. "I am so sorry, baby girl . . ." Ray's palms are clammy as he slowly raises the axe above his head. "I am a coward. I am sorry I ran away."

Bella lets out a wild moan as her jaw snaps open. Inside, the white teeth are stained red with pieces of flesh stuck between her teeth.

"Please forgive me," he chokes out as he takes a swing with the axe, violently swinging it like a bat toward Bella's head. Just as the sharp steel touches her cheek, Ray sees one final flash of Bella. His beautiful girl, still with her contagious smile. Always smiling, even in the toughest of times. Horrified by this, Ray closes his eyes tightly as the axe follows through.

Unintentionally, the axe is in perfect alignment with Bella's lips. With her mouth wide open, the blade slices through her cheek, continuing just under the ears and through the back of her skull, coming out on the other side. With a clean cut, the body goes completely limp, collapsing to the ground. Half of her head lands just beside the body as her brains leak out.

What only took a few seconds feels like an eternity. Slowly, Ray opens his eyes, dropping the axe in horror at how the slice was made. His heart pounds away at his chest, his stomach churning at the sight of Bella's body. Ray breathes heavily as he feels panic forming. That is, until a strange feeling flows through his body. Almost like there is some relief, a comfort in knowing that his daughter is no longer cursed to walk the earth.

Ray can swear that he hears Bella's soft voice talking to him, telling him, "It's okay to cry, Daddy."

Chapter 19

"Shit! Shit! Shit!" a young male yells out while running as fast as he humanly can.

Shane, age twenty-three, has been lying low at the Water's Bluff giftshop. The smaller shop's sole purpose is to serve as the ride's exit where employees try to sell on-ride photos.

While other stores are all equipped with doors, this one is always open, with metal sliders that are used to lock up.

This is probably where Shane makes his first mistake. He has barricaded himself inside the giftshop, leaving one metal panel open to allow some air to flow inside as the office-sized shop is incredibly hot. The open panel is the one facing the end of Water's Bluff.

Strategically, it makes sense, as anything coming his way will have to cross the ride's platform, giving him time to react.

It is definitely safer than where he was when this all

started: in the middle of riding the Ghostly Estate ride with his thirteen-year-old niece. A neat little ride that takes its riders through a house filled with ghoulish animatronics and ghostly apparitions created with smoke and mirrors.

Shane agreed to take his niece, Danielle, on the ride while his sister waited outside to feed the newest addition to her family.

The ride starts off fine. Everyone is brought into a room while a story plays, distracting you as the elevator brings you up toward the loading dock, where a little hearse is waiting for people to board.

A few seconds into the ride and the catchy tune begins.

Twisting and turning, changing its direction, the hearse moves sporadically through the apparitions supposedly haunting this house. Shane and Danielle love every moment. As the ride continues, screams echo through the building. Considering this is the Ghostly Estate, there is no way to differentiate reality from recordings, so neither Shane, Danielle, nor any of the other riders are phased.

That is, until the power goes off. Each car on the ride comes to a complete stop, unexpectedly jolting its riders, leaving everyone inside the ride in complete darkness.

"Who turned off the lights?!" one rider yells out from a few cars back, causing a small reaction of laughter from a couple of other cars.

"Your mom!" another random rider yells out, trying to be funny.

One. Two. Three more bloodcurdling screams are heard from just outside the ride's building. This time, it is easy to tell that it has nothing to do with the ride itself.

Shane and Danielle jump as chills roll down their spines. "What's going on?" Danielle asks with confusion as the emergency lights kick in, illuminating a safe pathway toward the emergency exits.

"Must be a power outage. Maybe we should get out," he says calmly as he stands up in the car, noticing a few other riders doing the same. "Come on. Stay close," he says as he takes Danielle's hand.

About sixteen other riders have the same idea of getting out, while a few others decide to stay put until either someone tells them to leave or the power comes back on.

Just as Shane and Danielle get out of their car, mumbling and moaning can be heard from the car ahead of them. The hearse is gently rocking side to side. "Don't look," Shane mutters as they walk past, assuming it is some horny couple taking advantage of this power outage to get in a little naughty time. Of course, when you tell someone not to look, they're going to look and look, his niece does.

While Shane tries to ignore them and keeps walking, Danielle stops and lets out a horrified scream.

Indeed, there is a couple inside the car, only they are not doing the dirty.

Hanging partially out of the hearse is a man, his neck broken. His eyes are wide open and bloodshot, while blood drips from a hole in his mouth where his tongue used to rest. On top of him is his girlfriend, blood dripping down her mouth onto her chest as she sits back up, the young man's tongue hanging out of her mouth.

A large, sadistic grin forms on the woman's face, allowing the tongue to drop from her mouth, back into the boyfriend's. She lets out a wild hiss, the grin on her face growing larger. The undead woman leaps out of the car, toward Shane's niece.

"Fuck!" Shane exclaims, taking Danielle by the wrist and running.

No one has any idea what is happening, but there is a crazed, murderous woman, and everyone's instincts are to get the hell out.

While Shane and Danielle run away, the undead woman jumps into the car in front of hers. The unlucky riders regret their decision to wait as they both panic. Their screams echo throughout the ride, causing further panic, forcing people to become rowdier as they exit.

Unfortunately, that woman is not the only undead patron on this ride.

Without any thought, Shane throws himself toward the exit door, shoulder first, with all his body weight, his hand still clinging to Danielle's wrist. The door flies open, and Shane passes through. Tightening his grip on Danielle's wrist, he gives a yank to pull her through behind him, only to be a millisecond too late.

Shane is still holding her wrist when he steps through the door.

Shane is still holding her wrist when an undead patron leaps from behind, tackling Danielle with enough force to sever her arm at the elbow. The last thing Shane sees as the emergency door swings closed is his niece at the bottom of a dog pile.

Horrified, Shane as he drops the hand to the ground. He hyperventilates as a small, agonizing scream escapes under his breath. The world is a complete blur as the darkness of the ride is replaced with the natural light of the outside world.

Everything from that moment on is a bit of a blur for Shane, but one thing is clear. His niece is dead. He can only assume his sister is dead, as she is nowhere to be seen. As far as Shane is concerned, he is all alone and all he can do now is try to survive.

* * *

Shane's hiding place is absolutely perfect as he is certain no one will come to him for refuge, and he doubts any undead will make their way to him. That is, until the side has been set into motion.

The loud splash causes anxiety levels inside Shane to rise. "Maybe they won't come this way," he says quietly as he stands up from his seated position, picking up a baseball bat he has snagged along in his travels from the sports memorabilia stores.

He peers out of his open door, looking left and then right. Nothing is at the ride platform, aside from the water dripping from the bridge, no one is there. Then he looks to the river as the empty log car returns to the entrance platform. Shane raises a brow with confusion as he watches the empty log pass by. "Weird," he mutters.

As he turns around, he finds himself face to face with a tall, undead female patron. Both eyes gouged out as blood streamed down her face like tears. She slowly opens her mouth, exploring her blood-stained teeth as drool drips down her lips. Shane stops, just a few inches away from this undead woman, a foul stench wafting from the woman's mouth into his nose, almost causing Shane to gag. Shane stands there, perfectly still, realizing that this woman is completely blind.

Taking a slow breath in, Shane takes a step backwards. The undead woman twitches at the subtle sounds of movement.

To make matters worse, several more undead patrons are on their way. Low moans from the distance get louder as they charge the mountain.

Without any choice, Shane drives his baseball bat into the undead woman's chest, thrusting her away, allowing himself to get a head start with running. Without any time to even close the steel gate on the undead woman, Shane takes off through the exit of Water's Bluff.

"Shit! Shit! Shit!" he stupidly yells out repeatedly in a panic, realizing that he is compromised.

He reaches the control panel and ride's starting point, stopping dead in his track. Several undead patrons stood on the other side of the ride as though they are waiting their turns to board. The blind undead woman is not far behind him.

Shane enters the little boxed room, kicking the stool in front of him to barricade the door.

It doesn't take long for three undead patrons to cross the river, smearing their bloodied hands all over the glass. Each of them scratches at the panels until they finally crack. Little by little, Shane watches in horror as the glass weakens, spreading across the whole cubicle until eventually it all finally comes crumbling down into pieces.

As the undead break through, Shane lets out loud battle cries while swinging the bat at the group of undead, only to find himself overpowered. He flails in fear as he is pushed against the ride's start button. His battle cry transitions into blood-curdling cries of pain as his flesh is ripped apart.

Gears start turning as the ride starts up once more. The log plows into an undead, knocking it into the seat and taking it for a ride up the mountain. The others take the longer route, drawn to the happy-sounding voices that are seemingly calling them up the mountain. The cheery music drowns out Shane's cries for help.

Chapter 20

Their moans reverberate throughout the mountain as they make their way up toward the top. Some of them stop at some puppets, savagely ripping them off their base as they mistake them for their prey.

A cute little squirrel dances alongside some beavers, while flowers twirl around happily. As the squirrel spins, a small undead child rips its head off. The metal body continues dancing as small sparks flicker from its dismembered neck. The undead child drops the squirrel's head with a low hiss as he rejoins the hoard, walking toward the light.

* * *

Tyler, Adrian, Steve, Katie, Jeremy, and Michael are sitting around, trying to decide what their next move is going to be. Should they stay here? Move on? Escape or keep making this place their personal playground, where rules don't apply to them?

"I say we try and build an army!" Adrian says, stating her piece. "Those things took something away from all of us, so we should find other survivors and fight back!"

Tyler, the self-proclaimed leader of this group of rebellious teens, nods in agreement. "I totally agree," he replies with a smug smirk on his face as he imagines his perfect end-of-world scenario in his delusional mind.

World gets destroyed.

Tyler leads an army to victory at any costs necessary.

Tyler becomes the overseer of the wasteland.

Tyler is simultaneously loved and feared by all.

While Tyler is being worshipped inside his head, Jeremy, who is probably the youngest one in this group, interrupts, holding his hand up to shush everyone. "Do you hear that?"

Not too far from where they are, the sickening repetitive melody plays. Waves form in the water as the ride's car approaches. Quiet moans soon take over the sound of music. Their enlarged shadows scale the wall, transitioning into dark silhouettes.

"Katie, Jeremy, and Michael, you guys get the snacks!" Tyler says in a commanding voice as he tosses a couple of empty backpacks to the three youngest ones in the group. "Adrian and Steve, weapons!"

Like good little soldiers, Katie, Jeremy, and Michael pack up their empty backpacks as quickly as possible. Each of then stuffs the bags with as many bottles of water and snacks they possibly can, while Adrian and Steve join Tyler at the table where all their weapons are laid out.

Tyler is enjoying this a little too much. His has been

reality completely overturned by some fictional universe that he often hid himself in. Even when he is choosing which weapons to keep and which to discard, his thinking is precise. Naturally, he likes explosives, so the bottles of vodka, scraps of cloth, and a couple of Zippo lighters are the first to be thrown into his bag. Next is the carving knife, a hatchet knife, about four steak knives, and some rolls of duct tape.

The moaning gets louder as the silhouettes are lit. The undead group begins to run, having found their prey at the end of the tunnel. As they run toward the group, the log turns the corner; complete with a confused stowaway, its back half in the front seat, while it attempts to crawl to the back seat, only to lose its grip with every little bump and turn.

This is going to be a close call, but thankfully, Tyler is quick to thinking, almost like a proper leader. "You two, clear the car!" Tyler exclaims to Steve and Adrian. "I get these guys!"

With their options laid out on the table, Adrian picks up an "emergency use only" axe, while Steve chooses the cast iron pan. Each jumps over the little river to catch up to the log.

Inside the log, the undead patron lets out a hiss as it finally manages to pick itself upright in the log as if it is motivated by the scent of fresh meat. With twisted arms, the undead patron pulls itself up, reaching out of the log toward Adrian and Steve as it slowly passes by. Its once-gorgeous blue eyes are grey with despair. Its rare ginger hair is messed. Ironically, this particular patron has chosen to wear a light grey T-shirt that reads "riot" on it. Fitting choice of wardrobe.

With no time to waste, Adrian raises her axe high and brings it down on the undead ginger's arm, completely severing it, while Steve jumps into the log car, swinging the pan with full force against the undead ginger's face, twisting its head around to the side. Adrian then joins Steve in the log car, helping him unload the undead ginger into the river behind them as the boat continues on.

While Adrian and Steve are busy securing their escape route, it is Tyler's turn. Grabbing a bottle of olive oil and a hatchet from the counter, Tyler bravely (stupidly) runs into the incoming horde.

The first one to jump at him is the disappointed child undead patron who has torn off the Skippy Squirrel head. He lets out an ear-piercing screech as she reaches out. Unlucky for her, Tyler brings the hatchet right down into the undead girl's skull, splitting it wide open.

Tyler expects this girl to go down, so it is a bit of a surprise to him to see her still moving. Firmly placing a foot on the girl's chest, Tyler kicks her backwards into the oncoming undead as the hatchet is released.

At this moment, the secured log makes its way to its final ascent up the mountain. It is time to light things up.

"Everyone in the log!" Tyler yells back at the remaining three, who are still stuffing the backpacks.

As Michael, Jeremy, and Katie hop into the front two seats of the car, Tyler holds up the bottle of oil and, with full force, throws it to the ground, shattering the bottle and releasing the opaque green oil from inside. He then reaches into his pocket, removing a Zippo lighter. Igniting a flame, Tyler holds the Zippo dramatically before dropping it into the oil, which bursts into an inferno.

As things light up, Tyler dashes back toward the table where his backpack is sitting. He looks up to see a couple of undead, unphased by the fire, as they powered through the flames. Not having time to fight as the log is moving, he picks up two more glass bottles from the table and tosses them into the flames to try to slow them down. Both bottles explode upon entering the heat, splashing oil all over the ride, spreading the flame and filling the caves with thick black smoke that just reeks of melting plastic.

Running alongside the log, Tyler tosses his bag to Michael, before hopping into the log and taking a seat beside him at the back. In the middle sit Katie and Jeremy, and up at the front of the log are Adrian and her brother Steve.

Click. Click. Click.

Behind them, an ever-growing hellfire is slowly consuming the entire mountain's inside. Each splash of water helps the flames grow larger and larger, and as the flames reach the weapons table, the remaining bottles of oil heat up and within seconds, explode, sending glass shards throughout the room as the fire spread.

As the log car continues through the dark tunnel, the kids let out a small laugh at how close a call it is. All of them take a moment to catch their breath as the log finally reaches the mountain's peak.

* * *

The view from atop the mountain is nice. The sun is setting, its warm light dimming as a cool, refreshing breeze fills the air. For the short time the log spends at the top of the hill, things feel normal again. For this short moment, Tyler and the others can relax and take in the scenery. Well, what is left of it.

The log eases toward the edge of the mountain. Unbeknownst to the teens, the ginger undead from earlier was caught under the log back in the cave and is being dragged around the final stretch of the river. It isn't until the log tips forward that the undead ginger is finally able to get itself up, wrapping its arms around Michael's neck.

It all happens so quickly. Michael and Tyler's screams of horror perfectly sync with the others' joyous screams during the log's descent. Being the great guy Tyler is, he pushes himself in the seat, away from Michael, kicking at him until Michael and the undead ginger are thrown from the ride.

And as the log disappears into a large wave of water, Michael lands on the water slide, his spine shattering upon impact. Meanwhile, the undead ginger loses his grip on Michael, flying over the water slide itself, landing headfirst. Its neck crunches in between the shoulder blades as shards of bone break the skin. Both bodies make their way down the slide, like a couple of mangled rag dolls.

Everyone is soaked. The four teens up front laugh with a bit of joy. Tyler sits in the back, silently horrified. Not by Michael's death, but at how it could easily have been him.

Adrian looks back to check on the others, her laughing coming to a pause as she notices Tyler alone in the back. Before she can even say anything, both Michael and the undead ginger land at the bottom of the hill with a smaller splash, gently floating down the river behind the boat, leaving a trail of blood behind them. Her eyes widen with horror as she turns to the side of the ride to throw up over the edge.

Curious as to what could cause that kind of response, Steve, Jeremy, and Kaity turn around in their seats.

Katie screams, covering her eyes as she turns away from the scene, regretting her decision to look behind her. Though it isn't much, a quiet Jeremy places a hand on her back, trying to calm Katie down the best he can, repressing his own feelings.

"Holy shit!" Steve exclaims, his eyes locked onto the bodies like a gawker passing by a traffic accident as the log pulls into the station.

With her stomach completely empty, Adrian sits up in the seat, knowing that they have to move. Being the first to get out of the car, she approaches the back of the log.

"You alright, Tyler?" Adrian asks, extending her hand to help.

With a deep breath in and out, Tyler swats Adrian's hand away. After all, he is the strong leader. He isn't about to let a near-death experience make him look weak.

"I'm fine," Tyler replies in a cold tone, almost offended that she is offering him help.

Chapter 21

Ray stands quietly over his daughter's body as tears flow down his face, washing away some of the blood splatter. It kills him deep down that he has to do this, but it is the only choice. Between letting Bella walk around endlessly searching for flesh or ending this eternal hell, the choice is obvious. The only silver lining is that his little Bella will now be at peace, and Ray gets a bit of closure.

There is no way for Vanessa or Tom to understand the thoughts going through Ray's head, but as parents, they can at least understand that no parent ever wants to lose their child. Which is why they are both doing everything they can to ensure their boys' safety. No parent ever wants to bury their children, not that Ray is going to have the opportunity to do so.

Black smoke escapes from Water's Bluff mountain top as flames consume the mountain ride. Time to go.

Quietly, Ray crouches down to retrieve his axe from the

ground before rejoining Vanessa and Tom.

"You going to be alright?" Vanessa asks with concern.

Ray gives a firm but silent nod. Even though he nods to say he is fine, his face says it all. It is tired and worn. His eyes are clear from tears and mostly empty, despite the appearance of a small flame of hope. This is the face of a man who, despite losing it all, isn't ready to throw in the white flag.

He may have lost everything, but something inside is telling him to just keep going. To keep living for Maria and Bella.

The flames coming from Water's Bluff are growing higher and higher by the second. It is obvious that without control, it won't take long for the whole park to be consumed. Though, if whatever this infection is can be contained in just Whimsical Domain, then the cleansing flames will be most welcome.

Chapter 22

"*Is anyone there? What's the situation?*"

Ray, Tom, and Vanessa are so close to what they hope is freedom. And just in time, too, because they can hear the undead patrons behind them getting nearer.

With her boys held close, Vanessa dashes past the Water's Bluff ride alongside her husband and newfound friend, Ray. What they expect is an exit. What they get is a large horde of undead completely blocking the park's back gates and monorail station, having a feeding frenzy. Dozens of blood-covered undead of all shapes and sizes are each enjoying a feast of unidentified bodies.

Among the frenzy, a young undead girl in a baroness dress is sitting atop what used to be a security guard, elbow deep in intestines. Like a child eating their first spaghetti meal, she squishes the warm gooey "noodles" between her fingers, smearing their sweet "sauce" over her face before actually ingesting it. And while the undead girl is playing with her food, the radio hanging off the body's belt goes off.

"Can anyone answer?"

As soon as Vanessa sees what's around the corner, she immediately crouches and pulls her boys both in close, making sure they are facing her, even though, by this point, it is a little redundant. These boys are already in for years of therapy.

"Tom, the radio," Ray says, pointing to the undead crowd. It is a risky move, but the radio might actually be the help they've been looking for.

On the left, two undead patrons, each with a part of intestines in their mouth, are almost recreating that famous scene from that cat movie where the couple share a nice noodle dinner. Only, instead of noodles, it is human intestines, and instead of a sweet kiss at the end, they have entered a game of tug of war to see who will get the last bite.

On the right, an undead patron is missing its left leg and half its face. Yet, that doesn't stop it from enjoying its meal of someone's arm. It probably doesn't even know that it is missing limbs of its own. Good for him!

And, naturally, behind the undead girl are several dozen others, walking, eating, and completely obstructing their path and ruling that exit, along with the path to the mono-rail station, un-usable.

All is not lost, though, as Tom points to option three, the docks.

The large lake that sits between this park and Creatures Domain. Just at its docks, there is a large empty space where the ferry is usually docked. Beside it are a couple row boats, floating gently on the water's waves, with no one near them.

Though it isn't the most ideal, this is their safest choice.

"Think they can swim?" Ray asks, noting that there aren't any undead patrons hanging around the water.

"Why don't you try asking them?" Tom replies sarcastically.

Ray rolls his eyes at Tom.

"Take the boys to the boat," Tom says, trying to get his wife and kids to safety. "I'll be right behind you."

Vanessa shakes her head. He gave her that speech last time, and he nearly got his ass killed. It is obvious that he is going to help Ray go for the radio. Though her husband has the strength, she is a bit nimbler on her feet. If anything goes wrong, there is no way her husband is out-powering so many undead, even with Ray's help. However, if it is her, she may have a better chance of outrunning them.

"No," she says firmly to her husband, knowing that he is only trying to do what he thinks is best. "You take Josh and Aiden to the boat."

Tom turns his attention to his wife, completely thrown off by this. He approaches her just as she stands from a crouched position, the twins both still keeping close to their mother. The shorter woman stares up at her husband with a look that just yells that she is not taking no for an answer.

"Ray, watch my back," Vanessa states firmly as she struts past Tom, leaving him with the kids for once. And before Tom can even object, Vanessa is already tiptoeing her way into the crowd of undead. Tom lets out a huffed voice of defeat as he watches his wife move.

Ray gives a quick shrug to Tom as he turns to join Vanessa on this mission to retrieve the radio. If there is anything Ray knows, it is that it is always best to stay out of a couple's arguments. Hell, he lived by the "happy wife, happy life" motto when Maria was alive.

Off in the distance, loud screaming can be heard.

With no time to waste, Tom effortlessly picks up both Aiden and Joshua, holding on tight with one arm each. His heart completely pounds as he dashes toward the docks. He hates that he is leaving his wife behind at the moment, but he knows deep down that she is a stronger woman than she appears. Definitely the smartest woman he knows. That's why he married her.

Chapter 23

Leading the charge from the now-blazing inferno that was once called Water's Bluff, Tyler runs at top speed with an axe held high as he flails the weapon around at anything that even remotely comes close to him. An undead boy? Boom! The butt of the axe handle is shoved viciously into the undead boy's face, breaking his nose and knocking him clean on his back. Another undead patron from behind? Just a swift swing as he turns slightly, and that undead is met with a blade through the chest.

It is a scene like no other. Tyler has just entered full adrenalin mode as reality takes a second seat to the delusional game world playing inside his head.

While Tyler is acting like a suicidal maniac, Adrian, Steve, Jeremy, and Katie are following close behind.

The group breaks through the horde, but they are not at all in the clear. As the teens are running toward the harbour, several dozen undead patrons start catching up. Leading the pack is an undead couple, clearly there celebrating their honeymoon.

The undead bride and groom are each wearing Skippy-World-themed shirts that say "Just married." And on their heads, cute couples' Skippy Squirrel ears, one made for a bride and the other for a groom. This probably isn't the honeymoon the newlyweds expected, but at least in death they are not parted.

The undead bride, slightly ahead of the group, lunges toward the cluster of teens. She swings her arms wildly and takes a leap, this time getting hold of Katie by the legs as the bride stumbles, then falls to the ground.

Adrian looks back as she sees Katie falling. She contemplates helping, but is stopped by her brother, who takes her hand, pulling her along with him.

"It's too late!" Steve says, dragging his big sister away from the scene.

Katie lands with a loud thud. She screams as the undead bride climbs atop her, digging Skippy-World-themed acrylics nails deep into Katie's back as she rips away at Katie's flesh. Within seconds, though, Katie shrieks, then her cries for help are silenced.

Shivers travel up Adrian's spine as she glimpses what just occurred to their newly made friend. Steve is right; even if they stop to help, nothing can be done. The moment Katie fell, she was already dead. A sad call to make, but a realistic one when trying to survive.

* * *

Vanessa is easing in on the undead girl that is on top of the dead security woman, her eyes focused on the radio. It is just lying there on the ground in the small pool of blood oozing out of the security guard. All Vanessa has to do is reach and run. That is it.

Taking a slow breath in, Vanessa reaches toward the black piece of plastic, getting down on her hands and knees. With her fingers stretched out, she barely touches the radio. She's so close. Everything is going well until a group of screaming teenagers comes running into the scene.

Startled, the undead girl drops the human meat from her mouth, finally noticing the not-so-dead Vanessa. The undead girl lets out a low hiss as she crawls off the security guard, thrusting herself at Vanessa.

Vanessa scrambles to her feet, pulling her arm as she narrowly avoids getting a chunk of forearm removed. But that isn't enough to stop the inertia of the undead girl, who is still making a beeline for Vanessa. She stands her ground, facing the undead girl as the space between them grows smaller.

The undead girl can just taste her new prey's fear, the salty sweat seasoning her skin. The undead girl can practically touch Vanessa, till suddenly, everything stops. The sharp edge of an axe pierces her neck while the blunt force of its swing drives the undead girl to the ground. Above her stands Ray, breathing heavily as he pulls the axe from the undead girl's neck.

With the undead girl out of the way, Ray picks up the radio with ease, tossing it to the now-standing Vanessa, who catches it with ease. "Go!" he yells out as the undead start to turn their attention from their food to the group of living.

Without a word, she gives a firm nod and takes off

running to meet Tom and the others at the boat.

An undead patron jumps onto Ray from the back, but with some quick thinking and manoeuvres, Ray throws the undead patron over his shoulders. The undead lands on his back and is then met with an axe blade to the stomach.

While Ray is removing his blade from the undead patron, another shorter undead comes from the side. Its arms reach out toward Ray with the obvious intent of ripping his face off. Seeing the undead coming from his peripheral, Ray gives one final swing of the axe. It hits the undead in the side of the chest, lodging itself right between the ribs, the axe head coming loose from its wooden handle.

The undead patron goes down, taking the metal axe head with it, leaving Ray with nothing but a short piece of wood to defend himself from the horde.

Seeing Vanessa reach the boat safely, Ray knows it's his turn to try to make an escape. He doesn't have to try to get away, but something inside him is pushing him, telling him he needs to keep going. And keep going, he does.

* * *

While he is running, Tyler feels himself slowing down, but he isn't about to show any form of weakness or allow these undead things to get him. So, in natural gaming fashion, he slides his backpack from his back around to his front. Reaching into the bag, Tyler feels around until he finds one of the bottles of vodka. Knowing that there will be more undead to come, he pulls the bottle out, opens it and pours a little trail as he runs.

Stopping for just a moment, Tyler rips a piece of his

shirt and stuffs the cloth into the bottle. Aiden, Steve, and Jeremy run past him as he lights up the cloth and smashes the bottle on the ground before lighting things up again and returning to a sprint.

Several undead patrons go up in flame, emitting ear-piercing shrieks as their bodies burn and their skin melts. Some of them go down right on the spot, while others continue their chase completely on fire.

One of them actually catches up to Tyler. The undead patron stretching its arm out, reaching and grabbing toward Tyler. Its breath, if it has one, is practically against the back of Tyler's neck. However, Tyler is not going down. No. Instead, as the undead reaches for Tyler, Tyler reaches for Jeremy. He grabs Jeremy's shirt collar and roughly tugs on it, pulling the young boy back and tossing him behind to the undead patrons.

Before Jeremy has any idea what is happening, two flaming undead patrons are on him. His clothing feeds the fire as the two rip his body apart, fighting over their flaming prey like vultures. Jeremy's screams are short lived. His charred body is torn in half as the two undead patrons begin devouring their halves of the boy's body, rendering him completely unrecognizable beneath the flames.

"What is that?!" exclaims Adrian, completely oblivious as to what Tyler has done.

"I think Jeremy tripped," replies Tyler.

* * *

A larger undead patron comes charging through the crowd at Ray. The undead man stumbles forward, arms flailing as he gets closer to his meal. With his neck outstretched, the undead man snaps his jaws in Ray's direction, so close to Ray the undead man can almost taste him.

Fortunately, just as the undead male is practically face to face with Ray, the wooden handle of the axe is raised and shoved crosswise into the mouth of the undead man. Quickly, Ray swings himself around the undead man, holding the wooden handle like a muzzle in the undead man's mouth. Placing a foot firmly on the undead man's back, Ray presses his leg forward while his arms pull the undead man's head back. A few cracks from the neck and spine, and the undead man goes limp, the bones in his neck having splintered through the skin. Kicking the body into the oncoming crowd as a distraction, Ray lets go of the handle, taking this moment to make his getaway.

* * *

With only Tyler, Adrian, and Steve left, the small team makes a run for the docks, which is their only option. They take note that there is already a family in one of the boats and, not wanting to join up with some adults who are clearly babysitting a couple of toddlers, Tyler leads Adrian and Steve to the boat beside.

With no time to even stop, Tyler hops off the dock and into the boat, reaching for the motor and pulling on the string repeatedly until a loud rumbling is finally heard and bubbles start to form in the water. Just as Tyler starts to back the boat up, Adrian and Steve hop in, assuming he is just getting the boat ready. They are completely unaware that Tyler really would have just left without them.

* * *

Vanessa and Tom watch as the teens back up in their boat. And with the sounds of heavy, stumbling footsteps heading toward the dock, it is immediately clear what the couple must do. Originally, they had planned on waiting as long as possible for Ray to catch up, but with the undead patrons easing in on their only way out, Tom has no choice but to start the motor.

Tom starts up the engine. Water starts to splash and swirl as the propellers spin. Vanessa scans the chaotic scene as she unties the ropes, pushing the boat from the docks. She sees undead tripping over each other, undead on fire (and spreading it), and then, finally, Ray running and weaving between the undead patrons.

The boat backs away from the dock with perfect timing as several undead patrons begin their run toward the boats with a lust for blood. Several of them run across the docks and plunge right over the edge, into the water, answering the question: Can they swim? The answer: Not well.

Like lemmings, several dozen undead topple from the safety of the docks into the waters below. Some sink like a stone to the water's bottom, some bob as they flail within the water and others get some leverage to get back onto the docks.

Tom pulls the boat out about fifteen feet from the dock, just out of reach. The boat gently rocks on the waves, while everyone inside the boat nervously waits.

Suddenly, Ray emerges from the horde at a sprint. A look of full determination is on his face as he runs at full speed toward the dock. He races along the damp wooden panels, focusing on the boat ahead. As soon as he reaches the end, he raises his hands above his hand and clasps them together, immediately transitioning his run into a dive off the dock, jumping over the undead that are trying to get back onto the docks.

These waters are crawling with alligators; at least, that's what the warning signs say. But as of this moment, an alligator is the least of Ray's problems. As he emerges from beneath the water, he front crawls toward where Tom and Vanessa are waiting.

They pull Ray into the boat, his body heavy from his soaking wet clothes. The three of them are exhausted yet ecstatic they have managed to get out together. While the sun disappears into the night sky, the boat gently glides across the water, leaving behind Skippy World's Whimsical Domain, brightly lit by the spreading inferno.

PART 2:
Creature Domain

CREATURE DOMAIN

1	Parking/Entrance	2	Water Rapid Adventure
3	Aquarium	4	Aviary
5	Africa Enclosure	6	Safari Bazar
7	Museum	8	Monorail Station
9	Dinosaurs	10	Ferry

Chapter 1

Traditionally, Creature Domain is the least visited park of the Skippy World parks. It's a fascinating park not only because it features exotic animals but it's also split into sections to feature the parts of the world these animals come from. This separates it from everyday zoos, creating a unique experience that most people living in North America won't usually get. However, no amount of Skippy World whimsey can hide the fact that the sole purpose of this park is to educate.

Do they really expect people to learn while on vacation? What kind of bullshit is that?!

* * *

Just like in Whimsical Domain, the day starts off pretty normal.

The petting zoo is filled with your usual mix of children

who are either excited at the idea of feeding a goat or just absolutely terrified that the cute, grey, exploited farm animal is going to bite their hand off. All while the parents stand back and record their interactions.

Scattered around the park, animal mascots pose endlessly for photos with children and children at heart. While their costumed expressions are frozen in ever-lasting smiles, it is safe to assume the underpaid employees under the mask are counting down the minutes till their first break.

Over at the Africa enclosure, an open-windowed bus drives through the dusty terrain. To the right of the bus, a young lion cub pounces onto what we can only assume is its mother. Though the lioness does not react, the young cub tries to get her attention by headbutting and playfully biting her. To the left, a couple of zebras are gathered around a watering hole while a giraffe rests quietly in the shadow of a tree. Obviously, there are walls around the enclosures to prevent the animals from eating each other. Can't have the animals going too *National Geographic* on us.

Three buildings form a perfect circle in the centre of the park, each connected by glass hallways. The aquarium, where for the low price of fifty dollars, families can throw a fish into a captive dolphin's mouth in exchange for a few tricks and a poorly shot picture. The aviary, known for its tropical enclosure filled with hundreds of exotic birds with a small, darkened section dedicated to bats and several types of creepy crawlers. And finally, the Extinction Experience; the park which is dedicated to animals of the world's past.

In the centre of the buildings is a dino-themed playground, complete with a Pterodactyl swing set (which kids are usually fighting over), stepping stones that are perfect for "the floor is lava" game and, of course, the slide that exits out a T-Rex's mouth. Because what parent doesn't want to spend hundreds of dollars to get into an amusement park just to have their children play on a glorified themed playground?

* * *

Placing his feet up on a desk, not even caring about the dirt on the bottom of his black tactical boots, a somewhat fit security guard leans back in his chair. Placing his hands behind his shiny bald head, he sinks himself comfortably into his seat. Pinned to the pocket of his brown uniform shirt is a nametag that reads "Senior Security Officer John Clemens."

On the desk are four computer monitors, all of which display videos that endlessly switch between numerous angles of Creature Domain.

Most days are quiet. Typically, the most "action" seen at the park will be some punk teenager thinking he can get away with stealing or a disgruntled parent upset because a worker accidentally put ketchup on their hotdog. And most of the time, it is the other on-duty security guards who deal with them. John usually mans the cameras, does the paperwork, and takes calls from park staff, after which he radios his underlings to check out the scenario. As a retired vet who has done his time serving his country, John finds this a nice change of pace compared to some of the action he saw back in his military days, serving in Afghanistan (which might explain some of the grey hairs growing in his beard).

John lets out a small, bored huff as he sits himself up

straight, removing his feet from the desk. With his hand placed on the mouse, he begins clicking through the feeds of the many cameras stationed throughout the park.

"People in line Jungle River Rapids.

"Monorail arriving at station from Whimsical Dominion

"Vomiting child. Tw— . . . three vomiting children.

"Mother picking out a shirt for her child. You better pay for that . . ." John mumbles to himself, looking at the clock, noting that it is only a little past ten.

Just as John thinks it is going to be another slow day, he comes across a woman on the ground with her service dog hovering around her. Its "Please Do Not Pet – Working" vest blocks the camera's view of the woman. Fainting from low blood sugar or dehydration is actually one of the most common occurrences at the park, so this is far from anything shocking and new to John.

"Can I get someone over to the Safari Shop?" John says with a bit of concern in his voice as he speaks into his walkie. "There is a patron downed and in possible need of medical attention."

"Copy that," a female voice replies. "Marcus and I are close by."

Setting the walkie down, John places his hand back on the computer mouse, clicking around, changing the camera angles to get a better view of the situation.

In one scene, he sees an employee in the shop, clearly frightened and unsure of what to do. John curiously arches a brow as he observes the employee. He is certain they have been trained on how to handle small medical situations. Freaking out is not part of that training.

Another click and the screen reveals a customer dropping their stuff and running away from the scene as quickly as possible.

"What the fuck?" John mutters as another angle shows a somewhat better view of the golden retriever on top of its owner. Zooming in, the camera focuses. The blurred image of a distressed dog trying to help its friend changes into a sharpened image of a bloodthirsty animal nose-deep in its owner's face. It is like one of those dog food commercials. One moment, the dog lifts its head from the "bowl of food" to lick its nose, and the next, it's back to savagely eating from the "bowl" like no one has fed it all day.

Suddenly, John's pocket vibrates as a little jingle begins to play. His first call of the day.

"Security, John speaking."

His eyes are locked on the golden retriever service dog eating his owner. The voice on the phone updates him about the attacks happening over at Whimsical Dominion.

John sees the security guard and medic he has called for enter the frame, both of them cautiously approaching.

"You can't be serious? Wait . . ." John replies, his attention glued to the monitors. His gut churns as he realizes this isn't some prank from the other park, and it is clearly not an isolated incident.

The service dog takes notice of the pair approaching. It pulls its nose from its owner's face, chewing on some cartilage as it takes an aggressive stance. The security guard pulls out a gun and starts shooting as the dog pounces him, knocking him down to the ground for the attack.

The medic screams as he tries to pull the dog off the

security guard. His actions prove useless as he fails to get a grip on the canine, his fingers slipping through its fur as the rabid beast flails about.

"I've got to go!" John states with urgency, ending the call and realizing his day isn't going to be so boring after all.

Chapter 2

With how closed off these parks are to the world, there is no surprise as to how rapidly this is spread. All it takes is for an infected someone to hop on the monorail or ferry, then start the spreading process all over again. And spread it does.

Just like Whimsical Domain, Creature Domain has begun to fall toward the fast-spreading virus as children start attacking their parents. Parents start attacking park employees. And the cycle continues.

* * *

John makes his way from his little security room office down one of the plain white hallways. He is unsure what exactly is happening, but it is his job to keep the park staff and guests safe. As the 6'5" man walks down the hallway, he holds his radio up to his mouth.

"We have a possible ZA-338 in progress. Police have been notified. I need all security personnel ready and on guard," he says firmly.

At the end of the white hallway are two large white doors with a brightly lit exit sign above them, leading to the outside world and immediately into the park's petting zoo.

Every time John walks through the doors, he is usually greeted with the usual barn animal scent while sheep frolic through their enclosure as children chase them and the pigs just roll joyfully in what most parents hope is mud.

The petting zoo is the one place in the park that almost never has any trouble, aside from a couple crafty goats that steal the occasional wallet from some dad's back pocket. To John, the petting zoo is where one can experience innocence in its purest form before the kids became old enough to make dumb decisions and find themselves in his office, crying for forgiveness.

As John pushes the doors open, he isn't greeted by the usual happy children feeding the animals. Rather, disgruntled sheep attempt to flee the pen while an undead child feasts on the innards of a poor goat.

Like the asshole influencer he is, a young man stands by the enclosure's entrance with his cell phone out as he livestreams the child in the centre of the pen enjoying his meal. A sheep dashes past the influencer, its woolly white body now stained with blood splatters. The influencer tracks the sheep with his phone as it passes by. Behind him, a pair of legs in some dirty torn denim. Panning the phone up the legs to the torso, the influencer is met by an undead patron, staring dead into the camera. Before he can even react, the undead patron savagely bites the influencer's hand, forcing him to drop the phone. It lands just perfectly in frame for the influencer's fans to see him forced to the ground screaming for help, as sand gets into his mouth, causing him to choke on a mix of saliva, sand, and blood.

Parents scramble to get their crying and upset children out of there as quickly as possible. Some parents seem angered that their day has been ruined, rather than showing concern for the people getting attacked, like true Karens.

As the door slams shut behind John, a pair of fast-sounding footsteps are heard beside him. A large undead man, with his eye hanging out of its socket, comes charging at John from the side. Without enough time to draw his gun, he crouches down. As the undead man runs directly into John, he stands himself back up, lifting the undead man with him, tossing the undead man over his shoulders and onto the ground.

Before the undead man can even get back up, John removes his handgun, firing two shots into the hostile man's head. Usually, lethal force is not an option John or any of the security team use, but his safety is at risk. Plus, he is pretty sure this guy is already dead . . .

Within a couple seconds of the fired gun shots, loud moans and cries can be heard from around the corner. The only safe thing for John to do is to return to his office; however, one thing keeps him from retreating. A lone child hides behind a park bench, crying in terror at the top of his lungs. No parents (alive) in sight.

While this isn't the time to be playing hero, there is no way John can leave this boy alone. With his gun gripped in his right hand, John dashes across the petting zoo, crouching behind the bench to the boy's level as he approaches the bench.

"Hey, come here," John says softly as he reaches toward the young boy, gently pulling him close by the shirt sleeve. "It's going to be okay."

As John extends his arm, the boy reaches back, clinging tightly to John, knowing that this is a man in uniform and the only stranger he has been taught to trust.

With the boy now in his arms, John turns back toward his security room door. Only now, it's completely blocked by several undead patrons, all staring at him with bloodthirsty eyes. At the front of the pack is the golden retriever from the gift shop, its mouth dripping with red saliva while its blood-red eyes are set on John and the boy.

So much for returning to his office. He doesn't have enough ammo to take them all down, and with this young boy in his arms, there is no way he can fight. Right now, John's only option is to flee.

And flee, he does.

The service dog ferociously barks as it leaps into a sprint after John. Its jaw opens wide, then snaps shut with each bark it unleashes.

Holding the young boy tightly, John flees the petting zoo. Running toward what he hoped will be a safer area where he can set the boy down and actually come up with a strategy with how to deal with this.

Chapter 3

With the sun completely down, Tom guides the boat across the artificial lake. The eerily calm waters, starting to ripple as a breeze forms, carry the scent of fish, smoke, and burning wood. An alligator gently drifts through the water beside the boat before submerging itself in the murky liquid.

In the centre of the lake sits the ferry that helped connect the parks. A popular attraction which resembled an old ferry from 1907 known as *The Yankee*. While it is usually packed with patrons, at this very moment, it sits there like a ghost ship that is slowly sinking into the ocean. Small fires aboard the ship slowly go out as water smothers the flames, leaving nothing but thick black smoke. From the looks of it, most of the ferry has already been abandoned, and judging by the half-eaten woman who is floating face down in the water, not everyone got away.

Tom, Vanessa, and Ray are all completely silent as they

pass the unexpected scene. Vanessa even sits her boys on her lap as she gently rubs their backs, trying to keep them calm. "It's okay. We're almost there."

A leg slowly floats next to the boat and while everyone aboard tries to ignore the carnage, a large alligator snaps its head up from under the water. It emerges for only a second, gobbling up the leg with just the blink of an eye, before returning under the water in search of more prey.

Josh and Aiden jump at the loud noise, holding their mother tighter than before. Both of them just want to go home and leave this nightmare.

* * *

"You still with me?" a voice says through the radio.

"Yeah, we're still here," Ray replies, as Tom continues to drive the boat forward and Vanessa keeps her children calm.

"I've cleared the docks, so just keep the boat en route and look for my signal."

Senior Security Officer John Clemens is waiting, shining a light from a high-powered flashlight across the lake to help guide the boat to safety. The reflection illuminates the rippling water as the boat eases closer. Despite all that is happening, he has still stuck to his job, ensuring that civilians are kept safe.

"I assume that light is you?" Ray asks into the radio as the light catches the group's attention.

"Roger that," the voice replies.

As the boat approaches, John steps to the dock's edge. Being the courteous person he is, he aims the flashlight down low to everyone's feet, so as to not blind the family or intimidate the children as he reaches for the boat to help them get docked.

"You're the ones from Whimsical Domain? Is there anyone else?" John asks, proceeding to help Tom, his family, and Ray out of the boat.

"Couple of teenagers snagged a boat at the other end. They had a bit of a head start, so who knows where they ended up," Tom replies, looking out to the lake, unsure of which way they went.

John gives a nod to Tom as he speaks. He hasn't noticed any other boats coming his way and knows that the longer they are out in the open, the more susceptible they are to attacks. He can't risk these people's lives waiting for a group that may or may not be alive.

"Alright, keep quiet and stay close," Johns states firmly, instructing everyone to follow him.

Chapter 4

The Extinction Experience: Home to Creatures of the Past. Where people can come and learn about their primitive ancestors, look at shiny rocks, and, most importantly, gaze at the numerous dinosaur fossils and skeletal displays. And don't forget to visit Extinction Emporium for some glorified pieces of plastic on your way out.

* * *

John leads Ray, Tom, and Vanessa toward the Extinction Experience building, the only place in the park John knows to be secure. Quietly, John approaches the gigantic doors, knocking the back of his knuckles against the glass as he flashes his flashlight through the glass to get the attention of the current lookout.

A female security guard opens the door, allowing John and the others to enter.

The lights are dimmed, but not completely off. The room, usually filled with random chatter and giggles, is eerily silent. Groups of people are spread out throughout the main exhibit room. An older couple sits against the wall with a couple pillows behind their backs as they quietly read, while a teenage girl sits beside them with her phone plugged into the wall as she texts away.

Just under the T-Rex display, the young boy John risked his life for is sleeping peacefully among twelve other kids who are separated from their families. His arms curl tightly around a stuffed tiger.

While several people sleep on beds made of towels and T-shirts, others are lined up at the cafeteria where two park employees are cooking up some hotdogs and onion rings, despite knowing that they are not being paid for this work.

It is actually surprising how many people John and his team have been able to round up into this building to safety. There are at least sixty park patrons, five security guards, and about eight employees all gathered inside. Whatever John has done to get this place organized, it is definitely more effective than the Whimsical Domain employees yelling at people with a megaphone.

"If you need a change of clothes, help yourselves to some shirts and stuff from the shop," John says with a small chuckle, realizing the irony of telling people to just steal from the gift store. "If you're hungry, Eric and Jamie have the cafeteria up and running. Oh, and washrooms are down the hallway, if you need them!"

Vanessa gives a polite smile, turning her attention to her boys. Both of them look incredibly worn out but are holding everything together pretty well. "Come on. Let's see what there is," she says as she takes each of their hands and heads toward the gift shop.

"I'm going to see if I can clean myself up," Ray adds, heading toward the restrooms, realizing his damp clothing is starting to stink of swamp water.

While Vanessa and Ray head off, Tom hangs back, extending his hand to John as they finally have a moment to breathe. "Thank you so much for helping my family," he says sincerely, unsure of what he would have done had they not been in contact with John.

John receives the handshake, gripping Tom's hand firmly. "I'm just doing my job in keeping everyone safe. I'm glad I got to you folks in time."

"So, is there a plan? Are people coming?" Tom asks with a hopeful tone in his voice.

John shakes his head. "I haven't heard anything as of late. I've been told backup is on its way." He pauses a moment. "But that was about eight hours ago."

Though things in Whimsical Dominion had started earlier in the morning, the pathogen needed time to spread. Some people showed symptoms and changed later than others as they travelled between parks, causing a time delay in when things went to hell. Although the pathogen started spreading close to nine o'clock, that meant things didn't really become noticeably chaotic till one o'clock elsewhere in the park.

Tom's moment of hope completely disappears as John goes on.

"For now, this is the safest place. All entrances are secured and locked, with armed security stationed at all doors. We have food, water, and power. Until we hear back from the outside, there is nothing much we can do," John continues, a low, defeated air in his voice, wishing he has more information as to what is going on.

"You want us to sit here and wait?" Tom asks with a hint of frustration.

Placing a hand on Tom's shoulder, John gives him a sympathetic look, knowing this is a father looking out for his family. "I know it's not ideal, but there aren't many options right now."

* * *

Over in the gift shop, Vanessa is busy keeping her boys somewhat happy. Amid all the chaos, it is nice to finally experience some form of normality.

"How about this one? It's got your favourite animal on it . . . monkeys!" Vanessa says, showing Joshua the little two-piece jungle pyjama set.

Joshua gives a quiet nod of the head as he takes the set, runs to the closest mirror, and places the pyjamas against his body with a grin on his face.

While Joshua is busy admiring his reflection, Aiden is distracted by another rack of pyjamas. These are pink with the latest baroness with super-cool snow powers, Eliza, and her normal but still pretty awesome sister Anne. "I want this one," he states as he pulls a shiny sequined set off the rack to show his mother with an incredibly wide grin on his face.

Vanessa glances at his selection for a moment and shrugs. Honestly, she doesn't care what the boys want as long as they are happy. Besides, it is kind of sexist for the Skippy company to assume that the baronesses won't appeal to boys. Every store you go into it is divided in half. One side of their stores with baronesses, dedicated to girls, and the other side with the Vindicators, dedicated to boys. If her little boy wants to wear those pyjamas, who cares?

"Perfect! Let's go find something for Mommy and Daddy," she says, placing a hand on Aiden's back as she takes him over to the part of the shop with adult sizes.

Chapter 5

With the sun completely set, the park illuminates itself with streetlights, spotlights, and decorative stringed lights flashing all the colours of the rainbow. This is usually that time of day when families either prepare to leave because they are just exhausted or try to squeeze that last couple hours' energy out of themselves so they can enjoy the late-night park finale.

Despite the "lack of life" in the park now, it really isn't that different from the typical end of the day. Sun-scorched undead parents slowly trudge along the dirt pathways like dead-tired parents forced to stay till the bitter end.

Tyler, Adrian, and Steve enter the safari-themed bazaar, a small pocket within the park, with sand-stone roads, jungle shops, and street food vendors that line the way to its main attractions: the jungle walk and the safari bus tour. Both attractions take park visitors through different animal-themed experiences, both equally educational, whether people like it or not.

"So, what now?" Adrian mutters, kind of regretting her choice to follow Tyler as they sneak toward the closest food truck.

While the usual rule of any apocalypse is to not go out into the open at nighttime, their stomachs are grumbling, and with the sweet scents of barbequed meats and other tasty delights calling the trio's names, they have to follow. Despite the undead boy in a bloody, torn Vindicators costume sitting by the safari shop directly across from them, comfortably sharing the dead carcass of what used to be an overweight adult male with some raccoons.

"Food," Tyler whispers, quietly opening the back door into the food truck, gesturing to Adrian and Steve to get inside before he does. A tactical decision by Tyler to ensure his safety in the event the truck isn't completely empty.

The first thing greeting Steve and Adrian is the warm air from the stoves, closely followed by the overpowering yet most welcome smell of warm, salty, tender chicken proliferating the air from several slabs of meat that gently spin on a vertical spit. Steve's face lights up as he immediately goes for the knife to cut himself some chicken while Adrian raids the mini-fridge for some cold soda.

When there is no screaming or panic from inside the truck, that is Tyler's cue that it is safe. With a jump in his step, he enters the truck and closes the door behind him.

A small hiss escapes the cool can of soda as Adrian gulps down the sugary substance. The sweet taste of fizzing cola flowing down her throat helping calm her down as she feels herself becoming anxious. She isn't the best in situations that require quick thinking, which is probably why she is sticking with Tyler. Oblivious as she is about Tyler's true intentions, she is happy to let Tyler lead. As long as he is in command, she can keep the focus on keeping her brother safe.

"Not a bad hideout," Tyler says, proud of himself for finding a food truck.

"What next? We stay here till help comes?" Adrian asks with a hint of concern in her voice. While they are safe for the time being, there is no way they can stay inside long term.

Giving a small shrug, Tyler dumps a bag of fries into the deep fryer. "At least until morning," he replies as the oil starts to bubble and sizzle. There is no way he is going to sit around and wait for help.

* * *

The sizzling aroma of fresh fries and cooked meat cascades from inside the truck to the outside world, its strong fragrance riding the breeze. The truck itself cracks and pops as its equipment is put to use. The sounds lightly echo across the unusually quiet bazaar mixing with the scents, unintentionally gaining the attention of some unwanted patrons.

* * *

Hovering over the deep frier, Tyler raises the basket of fries up. "Who wants some?" he asks.

Bang!

Outside the truck, four undead patrons start hammering at the side as they attempt to get in.

Startled, Tyler flinches, tossing the basket of hot oil and fries into the air. The crispy golden potatoes become hot projectiles as Adrian and Steve are forced to duck for cover.

"What the fuck!" Adrian screams at Tyler as the fries land around her. Droplets of oil screech as they hit the cooler walls of the truck, bubbling into a mist. Luckily for Adrian and Steve, they have avoided the splash of hot oil. But Tyler? He isn't so lucky.

In his twitch of panic, he knocks one of the hanging pans into the fryer. The pan dives into the fryer, causing a much larger wave of oil to spill over the sides, like a large swimmer performing a belly flop. The golden liquid moves faster than Tyler as it scalds his left arm, his skin instantly burning upon contact.

"Jesus Christ!" Tyler exclaims as he finally drops the empty basket of fries. "Fuck!" He inhales deeply as he tries to wipe the oil off with the bottom of his shirt.

Bang!

Bang!

Bang!

The pounding outside the truck grows louder as the truck rocks, indicating more of those things outside.

"We need to get out of here," Adrian states firmly, looking to Tyler with the hope that he will have some sort of plan.

"No shit." Tyler scowls back to Adrian as he holds his arm in close, the skin completely red from the burn. Tyler takes in a deep breath before reaching for his backpack, knowing that there is no time to worry about a minor burn injury. He doesn't have any magic healing potions to fix his arm up. All they can do now is move on. "I have an idea."

"Alright!" Adrian replies with hope in her voice. "What is it?"

"Vodka or oil?" Tyler asks as he removes two bottles from his backpack, waving them in front of a clearly unimpressed Adrian. It seems that this is the only thing Tyler even knows how to do. The cocktails don't even help that much. All it they do is send an angry undead patron into a literal fiery rage until the flames break down the body. Didn't Tyler not learn that in Whimsical Domain?

"Seriously?" Adrian questions.

"I don't see you taking initiative!" Tyler yells back with annoyance. "Hell, we'd probably be further if you weren't dragging around that kid with you!"

As Tyler points to Steve, who is quietly trying to keep out of the conflict, Adrian raises her hand. Her palm strikes Tyler across the face. "Don't you ever talk about my brother," she states firmly.

Tyler is actually shocked by this response. He has other things in his bag, but they won't be good for causing a diversion. Games usually have ropes attached to nets filled with rocks that will fall on the masses or create a noise at another part of the map to lure them away, and while Tyler considers the possibility, this is the real world.

Wait.

While Tyler will usually get angry about being struck by someone, he is actually hit by an idea. They don't have to take them out. They just have to lure the undead patrons away so they can make an escape.

His head turns toward the front end of the truck, the

steering wheel catching his attention. This is technically a moving vehicle. It is a move he has seen hundreds of times in both video games and movies.

With no words, Tyler pushes Adrian aside as he rushes to the front of the truck. Sitting himself on the leather seat, he begins frantically looking through the glove compartments for the keys. No big deal. If the internet is good for anything, it is random tutorial videos and—surprise, surprise—Tyler has watched numerous videos on hot-wiring cars.

"What are you doing?" Adrian asks, almost afraid to know.

"Once this thing starts moving, we jump out," Tyler states firmly, placing two wires together, causing the engine to rumble. He lets out an excited grin as the videos have not let him down. "Pass me something with weight!" he calls back to Adrian.

The first thing that catches Adrian's eyes is a bag of flour. Without second guessing, she tosses the white bag to Tyler.

"Get your things and let's go!" Tyler says with urgency as he shifts the gears from park to drive. The truck slowly rolls forward. As he exits the front seat, he drops the bag of flour onto the gas pedal. The sudden force of the vehicle speeding up knocks the unprepared Adrian and Steve off balance.

"Come on!" Tyler exclaims as he stumbles toward the back door, holding his breath as he pushes it open. The moving truck creates some distance between them and the patrons. He glances side to side, before pointing to the left. "This way's clear," he says, sitting himself down on the edge of the truck and pushing himself out.

Naturally, Steve is the next out of the truck, followed

by Adrian. While the teens run off to the left, the truck continues on its trajectory through the bazaar, running over undead patrons until it smashes into the jungle café. The glass of the restaurant's front window shatters into thousands of small shards as the truck comes to a sudden stop, unable to push forward as several dozen undead patrons swarm the truck, completely fooled by the diversion.

* * *

"I'm done with this," Adrian says with an exhausted huff as the three of them stop behind a tree to catch their breaths. "Steve and I are heading back to the docks," she states firmly as she takes hold of her brother's arm, turning to walk away from Tyler.

"You think that's safer?" Tyler replies with snark in his voice.

"Safer than with you!" she replies, letting go of her brother's wrist to turn back to Tyler. All she wants is to protect her brother, and she is at a complete loss as to what to do. This whole thing is fucked up. "This isn't a fucking game and, unlike you, I don't have a death wish."

Steve takes a step back when Adrian and Tyler start fighting. Adrian is his big sister, and he gets that she trying to protect him, but he feels Tyler is right. He is probably holding her back. Because Adrian is too focused on keeping her younger brother safe, she is unable to come up with her own decisions.

It is also funny to Steve because they aren't even that close to begin with. Most times, she is the gothic one who wishes to be an only child and he just simply exists. With those thoughts in mind, Steve quietly leaves, believing it is for the best.

"You seem to be the expert here, so I'm sure you'll be perfectly fine on your own," Adrian scowls harshly before turning her attention back to where Steve is standing. "Let's go . . . Steve?"

Chapter 6

Steve walks along the jungle walk, alone, thoughts in his head about how his sister probably doesn't care that he is gone. Why will she? She has never cared.

* * *

Steve and Adrian's parents are happily married, and it is clear Adrian is the favourite child, as she can do no wrong in their eyes. She has an outgoing personality and is never afraid to speak her mind, and despite Adrian's gothic appearances, she is a straight-A student. Steve, on the other hand, prefers to keep to himself. He is quiet and hardly leaves his room. While his sister is constantly being praised by their parents, Steve is constantly reminded about how he is "a disappointment" compared to his older sister.

Steve and Adrian's mother is five months pregnant. Another sibling is on their way to join the family. While

Adrian shows her enthusiasm, Steve doesn't really care. It is just another child who never asked to be brought into this world.

With only a few months left till the new baby, their parents decide to make one final family trip. Just the four of them, spending time together before things change. Both parents agree that a few days at the most joyful place in the universe, Skippy World, will be a great way to spend time together.

So, like that, Adrian, Steve, and their parents pack their bags and take a five-hour drive across the state.

* * *

Fast forward to their first ride in the park: Outlaws of the Islands, a fun family ride that takes its passengers down a magical river filled with drunken pirates. All of them sing about how much fun it is to pillage and steal, sending wonderful messages to impressionable children.

Their second ride, Whimsey Whirl, is a teacup-style ride that whips its riders around in a circle. It can have easily fit the entire family; however, due to his mom's pregnancy, she and his dad sit this one out. This is a ride that Steve and Adrian can enjoy together. And like all parents, their dad naturally has to pull out the camera to commemorate this moment of "sibling bonding."

Slowly, the teacups move in a large circle while the individual cup cars spin in smaller circles, building momentum with each movement. As the ride reaches full speed, the car whips close to the ride's fence, where their parents are both standing and waving. Both Adrian and Steve laugh as they take in this moment and enjoy the ride together.

"Smile!" their dad calls out as he snaps what is most likely going to be an incredibly blurry photo. It doesn't matter to Dad, though; it is still a family memory.

Continuing in its motion, the ride whips around again. Their parents are still standing there, both of them smiling brightly. Both of them so relaxed and happy to see both their children together, appearing to have a good time. Both of them oblivious to the undead patron beside them.

Just like a camera snapping a photo, the scene before Steve and Adrian all happens in just a few shots. First time the ride whips them around, their mother is jumped. The undead parent completely wraps her arms around their mother.

The next moment, blood is spraying everywhere while their dad is frantically trying to pull the undead patron off their mother.

Another time around and their mom is down. Their dad is now trying to fend off a second undead patron while the first rips off his ear with its teeth.

Each time their car passes the fence, the scene becomes more and more horrific. By the time the ride has ended, they are gone. Both parents are dismembered and almost unrecognizable. Left in a bloodied pile on the ground while undead patrons feast on their flesh. The only thing surviving is their dad's digital camera, sitting in a pool of their parents' blood.

It is at that moment Adrian actually shows Steve any concern for his well-being. Her instincts as the ride comes to a complete stop tell her to get her and Steve out of there and find some place safe.

Everything happens so fast. People are screaming, running, and fighting each other. Trying to get out of the chaos is nearly impossible. Just when things are looking hopeless for the pair, Tyler and his girlfriend invite them into their group. At the time, they are the only ones who seem calm and have a sense of what they are doing.

* * *

Steve finds himself halfway down the Walk Through Africa, a long, narrow dirt road that weaves through what is essentially a glorified zoo. On each side of the walkway are rails that allow people to safely observe the animals in their natural habitat. If you consider feeding giraffes and being photo bombed by monkeys natural.

Stopping under one of the path lights, Steve leans forward onto the cold metal railing and gazes out into the fields. He always thought it would be cool to visit a zoo at night and observe the animals when no one else is around; however, among the silence and inability to see anything aside from darkness, Steve is left feeling underwhelmed.

"Where are the animals?" he mumbles to himself with disappointment as he looks around for any indication of animals. "I thought there would at least be an elephant or giraffe!"

He lets out a sigh as he leans his head down on the bar, alone with nothing but the thoughts running through his head. Part of him regrets leaving his sister at all. Even if he feels like more of a burden to her, Adrian is all he has right now.

With his hands over the railing and his face resting gently on his arm, Steve's emotions and feelings finally catch up to him. His bright blue eyes fog up as tears run down his cheeks. Everyone is gone. He never even got a chance to tell his parent goodbye or that he loved them.

Turning away from the railing, a shadow out in the field of trees swings by. Curious, Steve turns his attention to it. His eyes focus on the shadow ahead until it finally hits some light. It is a lemur. Just a cute ordinary lemur jumping from a tree, living and carefree. The park plaque reads: "Lemurs are known vegetarians. Their diet consists of leaves, seeds, nectarines, and other various fruits."

Smiling, Steve watches the lemur swinging through the trees. Moments later, it's joined by three more lemurs. With the smile on his face growing wider, Steve follows the family of lemurs along his pathway. He watches in awe as the lemurs fly through the air, their silver and white fur glimmering under the moonlight. The bright smile of wonder on Steve's face morphs into one of horror as the family of lemurs lands atop what used to be a peaceful giraffe.

Landing one by one, they instantly rip at the giraffe's carcass and shovel it down their mouths like this is a normal everyday thing to them.

So much for being vegetarian.

Chapter 7

"He's probably already got himself killed," Tyler says with agitation.

As those words leave Tyler's lips, Adrian's eye twitches a little. She stops in her place, turning silently to face Tyler. Her expressionless face still emanates an immense amount of anger, enough to cause Tyler to actually go quiet for a moment. He can see that underneath the layers of white makeup and black eyeliner is an ordinary sister trying to look out for her baby brother.

"You better pray he hasn't," she states, taking hold of Tyler's shirt collar and pulling him in close in an attempt to intimidate the taller boy.

"Alright, sorry!" he says in a very insincere voice as she finally lets him go. "Geez. I thought you people are supposed to love death and stuff."

His ignorance toward what it meant to be a goth causes yet another eye roll from Adrian. Just because she wears black clothes and makeup doesn't mean she isn't a caring person. While the rest of the world sees her as some weird individual who worships Satan or some other evil entity, she is still a teenager trying to express herself. Not to mention the dark exterior serves as a nice cover for Adrian's anxiety.

Suddenly, a fun, joyful song fills the park. Its melody is more calming than the upbeat parade songs that tended to play. It starts off with almost a twinkling sound effect that fades into some high-toned instruments that are equal parts annoying and enjoyable for children under the age of ten. And naturally, we are greeted with a familiar female squeaky voice that starts off with an over-exaggerated yawn.

"Good evening, Squirrel Cadets! Isn't it past all your bedtimes?" the voice of Shirley Squirrel says with a giggle.

"I know it's past mine! But before I head off to slumberland, I think we should end today with a big bang!" the male yet still high-pitched voice of Skippy says, adding to his wife's introduction.

Suddenly, the park's automated fireworks shift into place and begin lighting up the sky. Little rockets shoot up high into the air, whistling as they fly up above the park and burst into all sorts of shapes and colours, each more elaborate and captivating than the last.

Explosions of blue, green, red, and orange illuminate the sky.

Chapter 8

While people are settling down in the museum's main halls for the night, Ray is in the restroom, having finally changed out of his dirty and destroyed clothes. Seeing that there isn't much to choose from, he trades in his clothes for some blue dinosaur prints track pants and a woman's tank top with Shirley and Skippy Squirrel, surrounded with hearts. It is all that fits, and he doesn't care.

Standing at the sink, Ray splashes water onto his face and hair as he cleans himself up. As the cold water trickles down his face, he takes the beach towel he has stolen from the gift shop, aggressively rubbing his hair dry before bringing the towel over his face. Refreshed, Ray drops the towel into the sink and gazes into the mirror before him.

His eyes immediately widen in horror.

Behind him: Bella. Her skin pale, covered with blood and dirt. Part of her neck missing as blood flows down toward her chest, soaking her dress in the blood. Her eyes are watering with an expression of fear on her face. As she opens her mouth to talk, her head falls off.

Frightened, Ray spins himself away from the mirror toward where his daughter is. His heart races as he looks around the restroom, cold sweat beading from his pores.

"It's not real," he says quietly to himself, glancing around the room as his heart returns to its usual beat.

Everything is normal. No dead body. Just silver stalls, porcelain urinals, ceramic tile flooring, and low lighting. It is actually a dull-looking restroom that doesn't match the energy of the rest of the park.

Letting out a breath of relief, Ray wipes the cold sweat from his face, walking toward the exit door.

"I said fuck off!" a muffled female voice exclaims from the women's room next door.

"We're probably going to die here!" another voice says. "May as well have some fun!"

"*I said no,*" the female voice replies firmly.

It is very clear to Ray what is happening, and he is not about to turn a blind eye. Storming out of the men's room, Ray kicks open the door into the women's room.

Compared to the men's washroom, the women's is significantly nicer, complete with flowers and brighter lighting.

At the far end of the restroom, a gorgeous woman with pixie-cut black hair, wearing a pink tank top and black miniskirt, is pinned by an older man with thinning grey hair.

"*Get the fuck away from me!*" the woman exclaims, slapping the old man across the face.

The man creepily grins with enjoyment as the woman

retaliates. He leans his head in close to her neck and takes in a deep breath with his nose. "Why you gotta play hard to get?" he says softly into her ear, completely oblivious to Ray coming up from behind.

"Is something wrong here?" Ray asks, placing a hand on the man's shoulder and pulling him away from the woman.

"Can't you see we're busy?" the man replies, his alcoholic breath filling the air with each syllable spoken. "Fuck off."

Ray rolls his eyes when the man goes on acting like what he is doing is okay. And if this creep is going to act the way he is, then Ray is going to do things his way.

"I think she wants you to fuck off" Ray takes the man by the shoulder once more and pulls him away with more force.

The man is clearly agitated by Ray's interference. He is so close to getting a piece of that hot ass, and Ray just has to come and be the hero. Realizing that Ray has no intention of leaving, the larger man turns away from the young woman, raising his right arm to take a swing.

Even though this man has a weight advantage, Ray has agility. He ducks down under the punch, immediately standing back up to strike back with a fist of his own.

"Get out of here!" he exclaims to the young woman while he has the bigger man's attention.

As Ray speaks to her, the young woman immediately runs out of the restroom. The moment she clears out, Ray shoves the man against the wall, his body hitting with a loud thud. The man's head smashes into the polished tile wall, creating a decent-sized hole. As Ray steps to the side, the man slides down onto the floor. His head is absolutely pounding from the hit it took. He is clearly still pissed off, but being the "bigger" man, he decides to just let go.

"That slut isn't worth my time, anyway," the man says with a low scowl.

"That's him," a female says.

The young woman wasn't gone long, and she has managed to return with two security guards, John and a shorter security guard named Gerry. The two of them immediately respond to the situation.

Gerry reaches for his handcuffs, which are dangling off his belt, and approaches the larger man, pulling him up from the floor.

"There is a zombie apocalypse outside and you're seriously going to arrest me?" the larger man preaches as Gerry takes forces him to his feet, pulling his hands behind him.

"Just because the world is ending doesn't mean you have the right to abuse women," Gerry states firmly as he escorts the man out of the women's restroom.

Ray stands to the side, allowing Gerry to pass by before approaching the young woman, who is currently making her statement to John.

"You going to be okay?" Ray asks, curiously sneaking into the conversation.

The woman gives a nod. Her lush red lips form a smile toward Ray. "Yeah. Thank you," she replies softly, clearly a little startled by what has just happened.

"I'll be making sure he doesn't pull a stunt with anyone else," John says in an assuring tone to both the woman and Ray. "Is there anything else I can do for you?"

The woman shakes her head a couple times. "Just keep him away. That's it."

"Of course," John says with a firm nod before leaving Ray and the young woman alone.

"Thank you," the woman says, taking hold of Ray's hands in an attempt to show him her appreciation for stepping in when he did.

"No need, I'm just happy that creep is being dealt with," Ray replies with relief. "Are you here alone? Miss . . ."

"Hannah," she says, cutting Ray off and letting go of his hands so she can fidget with the diamond right around her finger. "I get separated from my fiancé, but he's out there somewhere."

While Hannah is uncertain as to whether or not her fiancé is alive, as she has not been able to contact him, she speaks with hope in her voice. She refuses to believe he is anything but alive.

"If he is out there, I'm sure you will find him," Ray says in a comforting tone.

Chapter 9

oom! Whoosh! Ka-pow!

The fireworks light up the sky and echo across the park. The noises catch the attention of the carnivorous lemurs, gathered together in their unnatural meal of raw meat, causing a panicked frenzy among the group.

Unlike the low moans of the undead patron, these undead lemurs are much louder. Each of them screams and howls before noticing Steve moving in the distance. Their instincts for fresh meat kick in as the hunt begins.

Steve can hear the warlike cry of the lemurs behind him. He doesn't even need to turn around to know that he has become their target as he changes his pace into a run.

The branches beside Steve shake as the tree-bound lemurs catch up with no effort. Leaves from the trees fall softly to the ground as they are knocked from the branches. Within moments, a lemur manages to get ahead of Steve, ferociously leaping from the cover of the branch directly into Steve's face.

"Shit!" Steve exclaims loudly as the adorably murderous primate flies at him.

The lemur's eyes are bloodshot and open wide, as if someone has given it a few too many coffees. Red foamy saliva is dripping from its mouth, and its front claws stretch out as it prepares to latch itself onto Steve.

With little time to think or act, Steve pulls his backpack from his shoulder. Gripping the straps tightly, he swings the bag across his body to deflect the incoming attack.

The strike from the bag is successful. The impact sends the lemur flying off to the left, crashing into a nearby tree. Its tiny back wraps around the tree's trunk before the limp lemur drops to the ground. Finishing the move, Steve threads his left arm through the backpack strap, throwing it onto one shoulder.

Of course, with one taken out, three more lemurs leap out from the trees simultaneously. All of them with the same expression of rage on their face. While those three are mid-air, a fourth lemur, from behind, leaps onto Steve's back.

Knowing that he can't allow himself to get bitten or scratched, Steve reaches his free arm around to the lemur on his back. Its soft tail brushes against Steve's hand.

"Please forgive me," he mutters as he grips its tail tightly, ripping the lemur off his back and swinging it around before releasing the tail and sending it flying off into the distance. With that one taken care of, Steve ducks under the three that have jumped at him, allowing them to fly overhead and crash to the ground behind him as he continues to run away.

Unfortunately for Steve, while running away, he trips, crashing to the ground with a thud as his body skids forward. As he is about to pick himself up, another lemur jumps from the bushes in front of Steve. With one loud scream, the lemur launches itself at the downed Steve, its teeth and claws out.

Steve flinches as the lemur makes its move, preparing himself for the end with his arms overtop his face. That is, until a sharp whistle through the wind is heard, and the lemur suddenly gets knocked to the ground. Relaxing a little, Steve peers through the space in his arms to see a lemur now pinned against the pavement with a knife sticking through its chest.

"Holy shit! Did you see that?!" Tyler exclaims with pure excitement that he has actually hit the lemur and not Adrian's little brother, having had no experience with a knife before and not knowing that there was a pretty good chance he could have hit the wrong target.

"Yeah, I did," Adrian replies, unenthused yet happy he didn't hit her brother. "Come on, Steve!" she adds as she appears from the shadows with a bloodied hatchet in hand and Tyler beside her. "We need to go!"

As his sister calls him, Steve doesn't hesitate to listen. Scrambling to his feet, he swings his backpack back onto his back and runs over to his sister, instinctively wrapping his arms around her and pulling her into a hug, as he has never felt so happy to see her.

"Not now," Adrian states as she pulls away from her brother. As much as she appreciates the sentiment and she really is relieved to see he is alright, this isn't the place for it. There is still a conspiracy of undead lemurs out for the hunt, and not too far off in the distance, the sounds of low moans can be heard.

Using the hatchet, Adrian points toward the end of the path where a tall glass building sits. "We can take cover in the aviary!"

"Good idea!" Tyler replies, actually giving a compliment for once.

With no time to waste, the three of them sprint at top speed down the pathway toward the aviary. None of them looks behind, as they can easily tell by the loud screeching and screams that the undead lemurs are hot on their trail.

* * *

Adrian reaches the glass door into the aviary first, frantically opening the door and holding it open for Tyler and Steve. Once the boys are safely inside, Adrian rushes inside, closely behind.

With the door pulled shut and locked behind them, several of the lemurs throw themselves at the glass. One after another. Each of them is scratching and banging at the door, desperate to break through. Unfortunately, even though they are now indoors, the three of them quickly learn that they are still not in the clear.

When Adrian turns her attention from the door to the boys behind her, she immediately finds that they are now cornered by a little undead girl with half of her face torn off. Her tongue just hanging down to her chin. And beside the little girl is a taller undead woman with pieces of flesh missing throughout her body that have been ruthlessly plucked from the bone.

The two undead patrons both let out low growls as they immediately charge at the three teens. Both of them extend their arms as they try to grab their prey. As the undead patrons make their move, Adrian raises the hatchet in her hand.

Using his backpack as a shield to deflect the older undead patron, Tyler takes the defence while Adrian takes offence with the hatchet, bringing it down into the older undead patron over and over again. Each hit causes the blade to cut deeper and deeper into the undead patron's neck, blood splattering with every strike until the undead woman eventually goes down.

While Tyler and Adrian are taking care of the undead woman, Steve takes off running into the aviary. The younger undead girl follows close behind him. And like a cliché, Steve takes a moment to look back, tripping over his own feet. He lands flat on his face, skinning his elbows on the cement pathway.

Almost immediately, the young undead girl jumps on his back. The only thing keeping his back safe from her ripping it to shreds is his backpack. Carefully, he slides his arms out of the backpack straps. He throws the bag and the girl off him as he continues to run, making his way back to Adrian and Tyler.

As Steve circles past his sister, Adrian steps forward with an exhausted yell and swings the hatchet down into the undead girl's head. Her skull splits open on impact, allowing the blade to slice through to the brain. The undead girl immediately stops in her tracks and collapses to the ground as Adrian removes the blade from her head, shaking the blood off the hatchet.

Suddenly, the trees inside the building shake. Birds start

squawking loudly. Leaves fall from the trees as several birds flap their wings simultaneously. Hundreds of them peer from the foliage around the teens, and just like in the classic Hitchcock movie, chaos ensues.

Hummingbirds, blackbirds, macaws, and several species of parrots and toucans all launch themselves from the trees and dive to the ground below for the attack.

"Mother fucker!" Tyler exclaims, just wanting a break from this insanity.

All they can do now is run. And run they do. While Tyler takes the lead, Adrian takes hold of her brother's wrist, pulling him alongside her as they run once more, each trying to evade the birds.

It shouldn't have been a surprise to the teenagers that the aviary is compromised. What is usually a warm and bright room where people come to learn and interact with the many species of birds is just crawling with death.

On the many circling pathways, bodies and blood splatters can easily be found. On a bench that overlooks a small habitat of water with flamingos sit the bodies of what used to be a married couple. Both of them are limp, lying on the bench as a gorgeous white swan pecks away at their flesh. Honestly, this isn't really out of the ordinary for the swan. Infected or not, one does not fuck with swans.

Holding his back backpack up above his head, Tyler runs to the other end of the aviary, where a set of doors leads to the connecting hallway that will take the teens to the dinosaur museum.

"God damn it!" he exclaims as they bounce off his backpack, making it to the glass doors ahead and immediately pulling them open and dashing inside to safety.

"Hold the door!" Adrian yells as she bats away at the birds with her free arm as she continues to pull Steve behind her.

Tyler, being who he is, continues into the hallway away from the aviary as the door closes behind him. It is every man for themselves.

"Tyler! What the fuck are you doing?" Adrian yells out before shoving Steve ahead of her to force him through the doors first.

Stumbling ahead, Steve grabs the closing door and throws it open. And unlike Tyler, he stands by to hold it open, allowing Adrian to run through safely and acciden-tally allowing one parrot to sneak through before pulling the door closed and locking it.

Thud.

Thud.

Thud.

One by one, the birds inside the aviary crash into the door, one after the other, smashing into the glass and falling into a small pile of dead birds as their necks break.

Up ahead, Tyler sprints to the second set of doors. The ones that lead into the dinosaur museum. The rogue parrot closes in from behind.

"Get down!" Adrian calls out in warning.

As Adrian yells to him, Tyler instinctively drops to the floor. The bird flies over top of him and with no time to correct its course, flies directly into the glass door ahead of him.

Thud.

The glass on the door cracks as the parrot's beak lodges

in the glass, the blunt force snapping the bird's fragile neck, leaving it dangling from the door like a Christmas wreath.

"Thanks for holding the door," Adrian spits out as she walks past Tyler to get open the door to the museum, only to find it's locked.

"Shit," Adrian mutters, pulling the door a couple more times before kicking her foot into the door with frustration.

Unsure as to how long it will take for other birds to break through, what they don't want is to be stuck in a small hallway with no escape. Luckily for them, it isn't going to come to that as a beam of light from the hallway shines their way. It is a security guard, Christina, a petite yet strong woman, making her rounds as instructed by John to ensure everyone's safety.

Chapter 10

Sleeping bags and makeshift meds are scattered on the floor. While some people are sleeping soundly on the floor, others are restless, unable to sleep, or just completely awake and glued to their phones. Nonetheless, it is pretty late.

Not wanting to disturb anyone, Christina quietly tiptoes around the people, leading Ray, Adrian, and Steve to John so that he can give them the rundown.

John is by the front doors, as it is his turn to keep watch for any more stragglers or potential danger. Beside him on the floor, handcuffed to the door's handle, is the man from the washroom, pissed off that he is being treated in such a way.

"This is against my constitutional rights, you pig!" he exclaims.

"Keep it up, and maybe I'll just toss you outside," John replies, not giving a shit about this man's outbursts. As much as he wants to throw the man outside, he morally can't do it. Asshole or not.

Christina approaches, gesturing the teens toward John.

"They came in through the aviary," she says as she passes the teenagers to John to take care of.

"I'm head security officer, John Clemens," he says, extending a welcoming hand to greet each of the teenagers.

"I'm Tyler."

"Adrian."

"Steve."

"Right, well, help yourselves to some stuff from the gift shop, find a spot, and get comfortable." John says, having said these words several dozen times before.

* * *

Vanessa is sleeping soundly with her two boys cuddled in closely, while Ray, Tom, and their new friend Hannah sit atop a large, fuzzy blanket. The three of them can finally relax without having to look over their shoulders.

"I'm head stunt co-ordinator at GDT Studios. Driven cars through buildings, been set on fire, jumped from tall buildings, but I've never actually faced a zombie horde before," he says with a small chuckle, trying to lighten the mood. "Though, I might have to add 'survived zombies' to my resume once this is all over!"

Gently placing his hand on his sleeping wife's head, Tom's playful tone switches to something softer. "Vanessa here works in finance. Just got promoted to branch manager two weeks ago," he continues, gently running his fingers through her soft hair. "Between the boys and work, she's the ultimate supermom!"

Hannah and Ray can't help but smile at the love and admiration they see in Tom's eyes. The small gestures, the way he speaks about Vanessa.

"What about you? What's your story?" Tom asks, looking at Hannah.

"There is not much to say. I'm a graphic designer. Just fresh out of college. My boyfriend, Marcus, proposed to me in front of Baroness Emberella's fortress yesterday and we were supposed to spend the rest of the week celebrating our engagement." Hanna's voice trails off as yesterday's events finally catch up to her. "We got separated, but Marcus is out there . . ." she forces out, despite not actually being sure if he is alive. At the very least, the hope and belief that Marcus is still alive gives Hannah the drive she needs to stay alive.

"What about you, Ray?" Tom cuts in, taking the pressure away from Hannah. "We've been together a day now, and I know nothing."

"What is there to say? I married the love of my life seven years ago. We have a daughter together. My wife passed away. I brought my daughter here, and you know the rest," he says as neutral as possible. While Tom still has his world with him to protect, Ray has lost his, and while Ray has somewhat made peace with his loss, the memories are still going to haunt him as long as he lives.

This isn't quite the response Tom expected from Ray, but there is no hiding the fact they have all had one hell of a day. It isn't just Hannah and Ray. Everyone hiding in the museum has probably lost someone, making Tom and Vanessa one of the few lucky ones who managed to keep their family together. As much as he wants to tell Ray and Hannah that he understands their pain, he can't. The only thing he knows is that both of them are stronger than he is. If something happens to Vanessa or the boys, Tom knows he will lose his mind.

"Probably best we get some sleep," Tom says, gently cracking his neck before lying down beside Vanessa.

Chapter 11

With the morning sunlight removing the blanket of darkness around the park, the sun's beams reflect against crimson puddles as insects gather above mounds of unidentifiable flesh. Undead patrons wander aimlessly, looking to fulfill a hunger that will never be satisfied.

Sipping his morning coffee, John watches a gazelle grazing in the distance, a sight that could only be described be described as majestic had it not been nose-deep into a tiger with fresh intestines tangled in its antlers.

* * *

The scent of fresh bacon fills the museum as a couple of the park staff have fired up their grill. While some people line up to get their breakfast, others continue to try to sleep as they haven't actually got much. Luckily for Vanessa, she is one of the few who actually slept. One of the perks of being a mother of twins is learning to sleep whenever and wherever you can.

"You awake, Mommy?" Aiden asks, shaking Vanessa by the shoulder with the help of Joshua.

"Mommy's awake?" Vanessa groggily replies, opening her eyes to her boys' bright faces. "Did you sleep alright?"

"I miss my bed," Joshua says, noting that the floor isn't the most comfortable thing to sleep on.

"I miss my bed too!" Aiden adds.

"I'll get you back to your own bed soon enough," she replies, sitting up and taking both boys into a welcoming embrace.

As the boys pull away from the hug, Vanessa notices an unfamiliar woman sitting across from her. Seeing that she has been asleep most of the night, she has unfortunately missed the introductions. Before either of them can say anything, Ray and Tom approach, each holding two Styrofoam cups.

"Black coffee for you," Tom says, taking a seat beside Vanessa, handing her a cup while Ray sits beside Hannah, giving her one of the cups he is holding.

All of them immediately take a sip, desperately needing their caffeine fill for the morning.

Chapter 12

On the other side of the museum, Adrian, Steve, and Tyler are already awake and ready to go. Adrian is a little hesitant at the idea of leaving, but she is having trouble staying still. Perhaps it is how confident and fearless Steve presents himself or the fact that she has seen enough movies to know that while this place is safe for now, something is eventually going to break through. Whatever the reasoning, her fear and anxiety lead her to believe that the best idea is to get moving.

With their backpacks stuffed, the teens make their way toward the museum doors, only to be stopped by John, who has just finished his morning coffee.

"Where do you think you're going?" he asks with his arms crossed.

"Out," Tyler simply states as he tries to step around, only to have John cut him off once more.

"No. It's safer to just stay here and wait," John states, not wanting to let a couple teenage kids go out and get themselves killed.

"That is complete bullshit!" Tyler replies with anger. "Have you even got confirmation that help is coming? I'm not waiting around!"

While John refuses to let him and the other two through the doors, Tyler decides to take a new tactic. Taking the chair that John was originally sitting on, he drags it out to the main hall, where everyone is currently eating their breakfast. If there is anything he is good at, it is getting people riled up.

He sets the chair by the T-Rex statue and stands tall in the middle of the seat. "Listen up, everyone! These wannabe mall cops think they can keep us all locked in here like prisoners! There is no guarantee that anyone from the outside is even coming to rescue us, so I say it's time we fight back!" he exclaims loudly.

Ray, Tom, Vanessa, and Hannah all turn their attention to Tyler as he yells out to the people.

"Isn't that the kid from the other park?" Tom asks casually.

"Is he trying to get himself killed?" Vanessa adds as she takes another sip of her coffee, before returning to a nice conversation with Hannah, having taken the time to get to know her. All of them are purposely ignoring the kid, as they have no intention of leaving.

John wraps his arms around Tyler's waist and lifts him off the chair.

Naturally, Tyler flails his arms and tries to kick John off of him as he's dragged down from the chair. Rather than yell at John to let him go, Tyler decides the best thing is to continue his "speech."

"What are you all going to do when they run out of food!? Come on, sheeple. Help isn't coming! We have to find our own way out!"

Shoving Tyler against a nearby wall, John's eyes narrow with anger at the commotion he is causing. "Kid, you listen to me," he starts in a very firm voice.

As John lectures Tyler, two people step up.

"That boy is right! Help isn't coming!" one person exclaims.

"We're going to die here if we don't do anything!" another yells.

Within moments, the entire room has people mumbling amongst themselves. People who are tired and restless go through the pros and cons of leaving. While the majority choose to ignore Steve, a handful of people actually stand themselves up and head toward the door. Twelve people, standing behind John, are demanding to be let out.

With a sigh of defeat, John lets go of Tyler and approaches the main doors. "Fine," he says as he takes a quick look through the glass before unlocking the door and opening it for the idiots that have decided the safest thing to do is to listen to a kid who's barely hit puberty and leave the only secure building. "Go get yourselves killed!" he yells out with frustration.

Smirking as John releases him, Tyler returns to Adrian and Steve, tightening the straps on his backpack. "Let's go," he says with a small hop in his step as he exits the building with the small group he has rallied together.

Adrian hesitates a moment, looking back at the remaining people in the building. Part of her wants to stay, or at the very least leave her brother behind so she can return with help. Pros of staying? She and her brother will be safe. There is food, water, and a place to sleep. Not to mention their chances of survival are greater in the museum. Cons of staying? There is no guarantee that people will actually come to save them. And if things turn out the way they did at the Whimsical Domain, they will be as good as dead anyway.

"Come on," Adrian says quietly as she takes her brother's hand. As much as she wants to leave, she is tired of taking risks. "We're staying here."

Tyler stops as he overhears Adrian tell her brother they aren't going. He turns and watches as she walks away from the crowd that has decided to leave. He rolls his eyes and mutters, "Stupid bitch," as he leaves the museum, following the crowd.

Chapter 13

One by one, the people who are easily swayed by the bullshit that has emerged from Tyler's mouth make their way out of the building. Each of them takes in the fresh air and sunlight as they leave the shadows of the museum.

In the distance, a couple undead patrons wander around aimlessly, while a couple of escaped meerkats are busy feasting on a plump pig from the petting zoo. Aside from the few dead bodies and blood stains, everything outside the museum is in the clear. Anything that is a potential threat at this moment seemed to be occupied, meaning that the teenage kid was right.

"I bet you this is some government ploy to control people with fear!" says a burly man wearing clothing that can only be described as if the Fourth of July had a love child with an inexperienced hunter.

"Oh, most likely!" a stuck-up woman replies as she

walks past the burly man with newfound confidence. "They probably wanted us gathered in that building for some sick experiment. The government is always pulling shit like that."

Having not been paying much attention to where she is walking, the stuck-up woman unintentionally stomps her thousand-dollar ruby-red heel directly into the tail of a beautiful yet decaying tiger.

She stops, feeling the soft squish of the tail beneath her foot, but lets out a sigh of relief at the fact that the tiger is half eaten and not moving.

"I bet you this thing isn't even real!" the woman says in a disgusted tone, kicking the animal with frustration.

Smart move.

The force of the woman's foot into its backside is enough to wake the tiger from its undead sleep, and before she can react, the beast jumps up on all fours. Its tail rips completely off, landing beside the foot that is standing firmly on its tip. Screaming at the top of her lungs, the woman turns back toward the museum, but it is too late for her. The tiger leaps onto the woman's back, sinking its teeth into her skull.

Thirteen more undead patrons—each of different size, age, gender, and race—come running from afar, drawn to the screaming woman like a dinner bell. Beside them, a tiger that used to be white and a pack of squirrels that are cute, yet the embodiment of nightmares. Their beady bloodshot eyes lock onto the crowd ahead and their adorable little mouths open as wide as possible as their buck teeth are exposed and out for blood.

It doesn't take long for the group to double back on their decision to leave, each of them going into a panic as regret overtakes their fearlessness. People who are just exiting the building immediately step back inside, pulling the doors closed while those outside scream and demand they hold the doors open. Some, who are closer to the doors, pull back against those inside.

Caught in the middle of this, Tyler is pushed to the ground. Rather than getting back up, he army crawls his way through the crowd, keeping himself low and quiet as he safely distances himself from the panicked people. Everything is playing out exactly as he envisioned it.

Chapter 14

At the door, John and a few others are still fighting against the crowd, trying to pull the doors shut. As much as he doesn't want to lock people outside to die, they made their choice. Unfortunately, while a couple people get their doors shut, John is completely overpowered. He is pushed to the ground, narrowly avoiding being trampled as the people force their way back inside, causing the room to immediately erupt into chaos and panic as no one bothers closing the door behind them.

First, it is the squirrels, scurrying through the half-opened doors, then it is some undead patrons, followed by the somewhat-white tiger. Forcing its way through the doors, the tiger lets out a loud growl as he leaps onto the closest person to his right, his massive paws tearing through the person's flesh like paper.

A squirrel dives onto a young woman, who is sitting by the wall with her phone charging. She releases a bloodcurdling scream as it digs its tiny claws into her face. Three more follow behind, scurrying up her sleeve, violently scratching and biting away at her skin as the girl frantically thrashes around, trying to get the rodents off.

A married couple accidentally backs themselves into the Stegosaurus display as an undead boy, dressed in an obnoxious blue shirt that screams to the world 'I'm eight years old today' approaches. The husband stands between the wife and undead child in a protective stance. The undead boy leaps at the husband while the wife makes a run for it, tripping over her heels and into an undead girl in a yellow baroness dress.

Gerry, the security guard, finds himself facing an elderly undead patron. Its eyes are completely locked on the older security guard. Cocking its head to the side, the undead patron charges at Gerry.

Thinking quickly, Gerry reaches for his utility belt and removes a small canister of pepper spray. He nervously holds it out toward the undead patron, his hands shaking as he presses down on the button. His eyes widen as he realizes his one mistake: making sure he is pointing the can in the right direction. The spicy liquid sprays directly into Gerry's eyes, giving him a light seasoning for the undead patron to enjoy.

Gerry lets out an agonizing scream as he drops the canister, covering his eyes with his hands. Now that Gerry is completely blind and unable to defend himself, the undead patron tackles Gerry to the ground, sinking its teeth into his face. With one swift motion, Gerry's nose and cheek are completely ripped off. His body goes completely limp as the undead patron sits atop him, eating away at his face until he is no longer recognizable.

Still by the doors, John pulls out his sidearm, holding it out. Beside him, the pervert from the washroom is still cuffed to the door. An undead woman comes charging at John, and his military combat training kicks in. Not wanting to fire the gun unless he has to, he uses the butt of the gun to smash the undead woman's face in, knocking her down to the ground.

Another undead patron comes from behind. John ducks just as it's about to jump him. Quickly, he straightens himself up and flips the undead patron over him. The undead patron lands on his back and is immediately met with John's steel-toed boot. John stomps down with immense force, smashing the undead patron's face in, until its head resembles nothing more than a smashed watermelon.

The undead woman that has been hit in the face pulls herself back up. With little choice, John points the gun point blank against the undead woman's head and fires a shot into her skull, instantly killing her.

While John is distracted, the man handcuffed to the door panics, tugging at the cuffs, trying to get free.

"Keys! Give me the keys!" he demands in a panicked state.

As the man is yelling, a curious squirrel climbs up the door frame. Once on top, it looks down. At first glance, it is just a cute little thing, but the second its mouth opens, revealing its broken, unhinged jaw, its intentions become clear. The squirrel leaps down, its four paws spread out as it lands on the man's face, clinging to him with a tight, suffocating embrace.

With his free hand, the man reaches for the squirrel's tail, yanking on it in an attempt to pull it off his face. His panicked screams are muffled by the coarse fur. Unfortunately, the tail completely detaches itself from the rodent, leaving a bloody stump on its back where the tail used to be, its undead body having already started to decompose.

It isn't long before the one safe place of refuge has become a place of total panic, as if the virus has just started its outbreak all over again.

The undead tiger lets out a ferocious roar as it walks through a fresh puddle of blood, leaving a warm crimson trail as it slowly paces around the room, as if it is trying to select its next target.

Hannah and Ray push their way through the crowd, looking for a way out. Behind them, Vanessa and Tom, each holding one child tightly as they manoeuvred between the crowd.

"I'm scared, Mommy," Joshua mumbles, with his face buried in his mother's shoulder.

"I know, baby. Mommy is scared, too, but we're going to get through this together, okay?"

Just behind Vanessa and Tom, the tiger approaches. It gives a low growl and lets out a huffed breath as its sunken eye locks on Vanessa. She doesn't even need to look back to know what is about to happen. Chills run up her spine as she can feel its eye staring her down. Holding on tighter to Joshua as they run, she braces herself for an attack. No matter what happens, she is going to protect her son to the bitter end.

The tiger lets out one more quick growl before going

into a run. Its massive paws pound against the floor, leaving bloody prints behind with each step. Suddenly, the tiger pounces at Vanessa and Joshua. As it pounces, Ray stops in his tracks to allow Hannah, Tom, and Aiden to get ahead.

Ray tackles Vanessa and Joshua to the ground and out of the way of the tiger, narrowly avoiding the large cat as it lands its deadly pounce beside the three of them.

Bang.

A gun is fired.

Bang. Bang.

Two more shots are directed at the tiger, causing little explosions of blood across its back. Almost unphased by the bullets, the tiger lets out a loud roar as it circles Ray and Vanessa. Its teeth are fully exposed as it prepares its next strike.

The tiger violently jumps toward Ray, its front right paw extended out for the kill. Pushing Vanessa to the side, telling her to leave, Ray braces himself, preparing for the end. He closes his eyes, as he can feel the tiger's warm breath against his face.

Bang! Bang!

The three-hundred-pound beast plows Ray to the ground as its body falls limp. Ray lets out an unexpected gasp for air as the wind is knocked out of him. He lies there on the floor, pinned beneath the dead tiger.

Placing his empty gun back into its holster, John runs over to Ray's side to help roll the tiger off him.

"You alright?" John asks as he sets his shoulder into the tiger and begins using his strength to try to roll it off.

Aside from the massive bump he is going to have on the

back of his skull from when his head hit the floor, Ray is lucky. He has managed to get away with no open wounds.

"I'm peachy," Ray chokes out. "Don't worry about me. Just go. Get everyone to safety!"

Ray is ready to call it quits, believing that this is where his story will end. He has done everything he can to keep Vanessa and her family safe. This is his time. He takes in a slow breath as he accepts his fate beneath the crushing weight of this animal.

Each breath brings the weight of the creature lower onto his body until he feels nothing.

Nothing but absolute freedom.

While Ray is preparing to die, Tom passes Aiden onto Hannah and joins John in removing the animal from atop Ray. The strength of the two of them is enough to free their friend.

Tom takes hold of Ray's hand, taking a firm grip.

"You're stuck with us, like it or not," Tom says in the most stereotypical fashion as he pulls Ray to his feet. While Tom helps Ray up, John walks ahead, taking full control of the situation.

"We need to evacuate! Please, come this way!" he yells, trying to get anyone who is still capable to follow him out of the building.

"Let's go!" Adrian states to her brother. The two of them have been hiding beneath one of the dinosaur fossil displays, safely watching as hell breaks loose. It is surreal how quickly everything turns to madness. If people hadn't been so stupid and actually listened, none of this would have happened. The two of them crawl out from beneath the display and weave between the people in the room, running as fast as they can to join John and the others to what they hope will be safety.

Chapter 15

Considering both the front doors and the aviary are compromised, the only known route to safety will be to exit through the aquarium. And while John is busy trying to wrangle any survivors toward the connecting doors, Christina is already up ahead, waiting, with the doors unlocked and open for people to pass through safely.

The steps of several undead patrons echo down the hall behind John and the civilians. Realizing they are not far behind, John stops in his path, allowing Ray and everyone else to pass him. Having already used the last of the remaining bullets from his sidearm, John arms himself with the baton from his belt.

"Just get everyone out!" he yells to Christina as he stands, facing the undead patrons with the baton armed and ready to fight to the end.

For the moment, it is six against one.

Using his baton, John strikes an undead patron across

the face, knocking it off balance. While that one stumbles back, another one jumps at him. John steps to the side and pulls the undead patron into an armlock. He swings that patron around and places his baton firmly around its neck, pulling the baton into the undead patron's neck. The undead patron's neck snaps. Its flailing arms fall limp as John kicks it back into the growing horde.

As one undead patron goes down, two more pop up. It is apparent that sooner or later, John is either going to become one of those things or become their meal.

Christina watches as John attempts to take on the horde alone as the civilians exit the museum and enter the aquarium. Just as quickly as Ray, Tom, and Vanessa run into the second building, Christina pushes the doors closed.

Click.

By the time Ray and the others can even clue in as to what has happened, the door is locked, and Christina is running toward John to help.

"Hey! Wait!" Ray calls out, pulling on the door's handle and banging on the glass in horror. His chest feels tight as he feels completely helpless. While Christina is doing what she feels is the right thing, not allowing her co-worker/friend to fight alone, all Ray can think about is how this is a preventable death.

Holding her sidearm up, Christina fires a shot dead centre into the head of one of the undead patrons. While it goes down, another lets out a wild hiss as it pushes past its fallen "comrade."

"What are you doing? I told you to go!" John exclaims as he bashes one of the undead patrons' heads in. Blood splatters everywhere as its skull collapses in on itself. With a smirk, John confidently wipes the blood off his face as he goes in to fend off another undead patron.

"You said to get everyone out," Christina replies as she fires a bullet point blank into the face of an undead woman. The bullet causes the face to explode into a gooey mess of blood, brains, and other fluids. "You didn't specify that I had to go with them."

John rolls his eyes as she points out his very obvious loophole. While Christina is a younger guard, she takes her job seriously. She wants to be a police officer, but the only job she could get after graduating from her Police Foundations program was as a security guard. She has a lot of spirit in her and is always willing to go above and beyond for her work. The safety of others is always her top priority, even if it comes at the price of her life. John can respect that.

Standing back-to-back, John and Christina find themselves completely surrounded, with no way out. Christina has no more bullets, and John's energy is quickly depleting with every strike of his baton. They both examine the circle of undead. It is clear that this is it.

"Christina?"

"Yeah?"

"You would have been an amazing officer."

The circle of undead patrons collapses in on John and Christina. First Christina is tackled to the floor, then John's leg is pulled from beneath him. He falls to the ground, his head smashing into the cement floor. Within seconds, the two of them disappear beneath the ever-growing dog pile of undead patrons.

Chapter 16

Of the original sixty-plus people who were hiding out in the museum, all that remain are:

- A widowed father who watched his daughter die
- A husband and wife keeping their twins safe

They are now joined by:

- A sister struggling to protect her younger brother
- A thin, pale, dorky kid with long wavy brown hair, sporting a fashionable Harold named Harold
- A forty-something woman named Karen, who appears to be about five months pregnant
- A quiet elderly man who is surprisingly fit for his age, whose name is unknown
- And Hannah

It isn't the type of group people consider when creating

their "zombie apocalypse team," but this is it. The only people who have managed to fight their way through the museum into the unknown horrors awaiting them.

* * *

The aquarium. It is a low-lit part of the building with several large tanks, which illuminate the room with a cool blue tone. Fish from all types of waters from across the world are divided into their own temperature-regulated tanks. All swim freely through the water, seemingly unaffected by the world around them, like the bats back at the aviary.

Calming music is playing throughout the building. While under most circumstances, the music will be welcome, all it does now is to amplify the horrific scene outside of the calm waters themselves.

On one tank, a bloodied handprint is smeared all over its glass. Below the print, a boy who can't have been any older than four. He is lying completely lifeless on the ground. A plush whale is clutched in his hands. Beside him is an empty stroller with a hand still holding onto the handles, but there is no body to be found. The grotesque scene paints a picture of what has originally started off as a parent and child bonding moment as they watched the various colourful fish swimming by.

In one tank, carnivorous fish swim around in murky red water while a body floats near the bottom of the tank. Its skin is grey as it has already started rotting. Most of the body's face has been devoured, rendering the poor soul unrecognizable. Bits of flesh are still being plucked off by passing fish.

An employee in a large fish mascot costume lies dead on the ground, his leg severed from his body while the foam costume around him has been torn to shreds. The employee's head sticks out of the costume with his eyes rolled into the back of his head. Behind the employee is the main lobby of the aquarium, with doors leading outside.

Just beside the employee, lying on the floor, are several stanchions with a connecting rope.

Ray cautiously steps over the dead employee as he leads the rest of the survivors through the building. He has no weapons. No plan. No idea what he is even doing, yet here he is, at the front of the group, accidentally assuming the leadership role. A role that would have been much better suited for Tom, had he not been preoccupied at the moment trying to be a good father.

If there is any time for everyone to catch their breath, this is it. Aside from the sight of death everywhere in this building, it seems everyone is in the clear. There are no sounds indicating any undead nearby, and the bodies that are scattered around do not look as though they will be getting back up. Some look like they have been laying there for over a day now.

"We should try to figure out a plan before we head out," Ray states, leaning himself against a fish tank to catch his breath.

Tom and Vanessa both nod in agreement, knowing it is getting difficult with the boys. There is no chance in hell either parent will leave their child behind, but trying to run or fight back is nearly impossible with the increasing number of undead patrons appearing.

Adrian lets go of her brother's hand a moment as she steps up to speak. "The monorails might still be running," she says quietly, unsure whether this is a good idea or not.

"The monorails are close by," Tom adds, knowing that they are out the doors of the aquarium and just on the other side of the Wilderness Rapids safari ride. "There's no way of telling if COPET is any better than here, but it might be our only option."

Hannah nods her head as she listens. "Whatever the plan is, I'm not leaving without my fiancé."

Ray goes to reply but bites his tongue. Hannah seems like a strong, intelligent girl, but it is clear she isn't set on the idea that her better half is no longer living.

Fortunately, the elderly man has chimed in with the exact words that are on Ray's mind. "What if he's dead?" he states flatly, not giving any care whatsoever to Hannah's feelings. Then again, it is the realization behind the situation.

"He's not dead! Okay! He is alive and out there somewhere!" she yells back at the elderly man.

"How do you know?" the man replies bluntly. "How do you know he didn't just leave you here to die and save himself?

"That's enough!" Ray exclaims, realizing that while the elderly man is correct, Hannah isn't in the best state of mind to be hearing it. Right now, everyone is hurting one way or another and arguing isn't going to help anyone.

While everyone has stopped in the aquarium lobby to take a break, Harold and Karen have continued on a little farther to take in the calming sights of the aquatic life, taking this downtime to relax in their own way. Both of them stop in front of a large take, staring at the ignorant fish, swimming peacefully in their artificial habitat. Currently living peacefully with the other fish, completely oblivious that their daily meals will no longer be coming. Unknowing that, like the world outside, they will have to succumb to cannibalistic intentions in order to continue living.

While Karen chooses to stay and watch the tropical fish, Harold moves on to the next tank.

Harold leans into the glass, watching as an octopus passes by. Its body mesmerizes him as its tentacles flutter forward, then extend back, causing the octopus to glide smoothly through the water. It is almost as if the water itself is parting out of the octopus's way. It is a calming sight.

Harold keeps his eyes locked on the octopus as it glides from one part of the tank to the next. Each movement more graceful than the last. Each flutter of the tentacles creating a calming sensation that makes him think everything is going to be alright.

Unfortunately for Harold, while he is mesmerized by the octopus in front of him, he should have been paying attention to the octopus that is halfway out of its tank. Its discoloured tentacle reaches down the side of the tank toward Harold. With a quick snap, the octopus wraps its tentacle around Harold's neck. Each of the little teeth in the suction cups sinks, securing themselves to Harold's skin as the octopus pulls him up from the ground below and toward the tank.

Harold screams in horror, alerting Karen to his situation.

Without thinking. Seriously. Without thinking whatsoever, Karen grabs onto Harold's legs, pulling against the octopus in a game of human tug-o-war with Harold as the rope. The tentacle squeezes tighter. Tighter. Tighter until Harold's face turns blue. His eyes bulge as he gasps for air. The vessels in his eyes are about to burst as Karen loses her grip, releasing Harold to the octopus. The tentacles then retract into the tank, dragging Harold's body up along the glass and into the water.

Karen's screams of horror echo through the aquarium.

"Wait here," Ray exclaims, stepping over the fish mascot employee and picking up a metal stanchion as a weapon.

Karen backs herself against the piranha tank, which houses the body of an unfortunate park guest. She is laughing, crying, and has completely succumbed to hysteria.

"What happened?" Ray asks, approaching the woman with concern.

Hyperventilating, Karen points to the tank behind Ray. Inside, Harold, floating unconscious while three octopuses fought over him. Their tentacles entangle around his body as they all tug as hard as they can in opposite directions. The joints in Harold's arms and legs pop out of their sockets as the skin around his neck tears. With one final pull, five clouds of blood disperse into the water as the octopuses each swim off, leaving nothing but the floating torso of what used to be Harold.

"We need to go," Ray states firmly, taking hold of Karen's wrist.

Just as they are about to make a break from it, a large splash of water erupts from the tank behind Karen. Hanging over the glass is the half-eaten patron who has been slumbering at the bottom. Its wet, slimy hands reach out and grab Karen's hair. With all its strength, the undead patron pulls her back toward the tank.

As Karen's hand slips from Ray's, her head is smashed into the glass behind them. The glass from the tank immediately shatters from the impact. Water, glass, and fish explode everywhere.

Splish. Splash.
Splish. Splash.
Splish. Splash.

Several fish hundred fish flop around on the ground. Splashing in the puddles, the unlucky ones narrowly avoid shards of glass with each jump. In the middle of them is Karen, who is completely soaked and judging by the red water by her head, very dead. Atop of her is the undead patron, freed from his watery grave.

With low growls, the undead patron digs his nails into Karen's torso as he pushes himself up to his feet. Water droplets fall from the undead patron's clothes as he completely stands himself up straight.

"Fuck!" Ray mutters.

Jumping off Karen, the undead patron lunges at Ray with murderous intent. Ray lifts the steel stanchion in his hand, swinging it with as much force as humanly possible. The stanchion smashes its way through the undead patron's face, just across the eyes, causing its forehead to cave in. The undead patron is completely downed, but within seconds, the low moans of other undead reverberate throughout the aquarium. Their temporary safe place is clearly compromised.

* * *

Karen's screams echo around the aquarium. The high-pitched tone reaches not only the group awaiting the return of Ray, but the dead as well, alerting them like an alarm clock that it is time to get up.

The young child in the stroller sits itself up. Snapping its head to the side, it lets out a high-pitched moan that joins in with several others throughout the building.

Even the employee in the fish costume moves. First, he twitches in his spot as he "awakens," followed by an attempt to crawl across the dirty floor using his hands. Immediately upon seeing this movement from the undead employee, Tom passes Aiden to Vanessa.

"Don't even fucking think about it!" Tom mutters to the undead employee as he picks up a stanchion and firmly brings the base of it repeatedly down on the undead employee's head without skipping a beat.

First hit, the undead employee is knocked back to the ground.

Second hit, the undead employee lets out louder groans as he scratches at the cement below.

Third hit, the undead employee's head is pulverized. His brains protrude through the cranium as sticky red fluids ooze out onto the floor, like a watermelon that has been thrown off a roof.

"Shit! Shit! Shit!" Ray exclaims as he comes barrelling through the aquarium, toward the front lobby where everyone has been waiting. Close behind him is the undead patron that killed Karen.

Not paying attention to where he is running, Ray steps his

down into the gooey mess that used to be a park employee. His foot loses traction on the floor, sending him flying right onto his back. His visual of the door ahead transitions into the high ceilings above as he drops his stanchion.

Clink. Clink. Clink.

The stanchion rolls away, out of Ray's reach. Taking advantage of Ray's temporary handicap, the undead patron dives toward him. Just as he is about to land on Ray, Ray brings his knees into his chest, extending his legs out with the perfect timing, launching the patron over and behind him.

In perfect tag team formation, as soon as the patron lands face-up on the ground, Tom steps in with his stanchion and smashes the undead's head over and over. Hit after hit, its face becomes more and more deformed until its body is limp and unresponsive. By the time Tom finishes, there is nothing more than a couple eyeballs staring through a caved-in skull and what appears to be a terrifying grin on his face with several chipped and missing teeth. Just like the fish employee, the face beneath this bloodied mess is beyond recognizable.

Dropping the sanction, Tom extends a helping hand to Ray.

"Thanks," Ray says, taking a tight grip of Tom's hand.

"You're stuck with us," Tom replies with a small smirk, letting Ray know that by this point, he is pretty much family. Since the beginning of all this, Ray has been the one person to step in and help his family, despite having lost everything. Plus, Joshua and Aiden really like him, so as far as Vanessa and Tom are concerned, he is one of them.

Shadows reflect through the water of the tanks, waving gently on the aquarium walls. Noises continue to echo through toward the group as they stand by the main lobby. The first of the group to make its appearance is the little boy from when they first entered.

The undead preschooler sees Ray and the others, letting out a hiss as if calling the more undead to his location. The undead preschooler runs as fast as a preschooler can realistically run with such small legs. Take away the murderous aspect of it, and it is almost laughably adorable.

Ray picks his stanchion back up, holding it in the air like a bat, and watches as the undead toddler comes his way. Taking a deep breath, Ray closes his eyes and prepares to swing away. Only when he opens his eyes, the world around him changes.

His wife, Maria, stands before him, holding young Bella's hands. Letting go of her mother's hands, Bella runs toward Ray. Four years old, wearing a beautiful blue sundress, which is flowing ever so gracefully behind her.

"Ray."

He can hear his wife calling his name, her voice ever so calming.

"Ray."

As Bella gets closer to Ray, he drops his stanchion and crouches to welcome the little girl.

"Ray!"

A hand tightly grips his shoulder, and with one swift motion, Ray is pulled from the illusion inside his mind and back into reality. The soothing tone of his wife's voice warps to the lower, panicked tone of Hannah.

"Ray, what the fuck are you doing?!" Hannah exclaims as she roughly pulls Ray toward the building exit, while the elderly man grabs the undead child by its armpits, tossing it across the floor. "Everyone's already left the building! Come on!"

Chapter 17

Outside the aquarium doors is a nicely paved cobblestone pathway splitting into three directions: left to Extinction Experience, middle leading to the docks, and right path to the Wilderness Rapids ride.

While Adrian, Steve, Tom, and Vanessa are already outside, each with their guard up and ready to move if needed, Ray, Hannah, and the elderly man are finally exiting through the doors. Of course, with no real way to barricade the doors at the moment, all they can do is keep moving.

"Monorail is this way," Adrian says calmly, as she takes hold of her brother's hand, pulling him close.

The group pushes forward along the park path, like a paranoid herd of deer, anticipating an attack at any moment. Leading the herd, Ray, who has pressed himself ahead, feeling responsible for the safety of these people.

In the distance, a body lies motionless on the ground. To everyone's surprise, this is the first dead thing the group has even seen on this path (aside from the few undead people hanging out by some other attractions). Taking the initiative, Ray cautiously steps forward to assess the situation.

The body is lying face down against the cement. Its humerus has pierced the skin and is pointing up into the sky. Judging by some of the decay around the skin, this person is probably undead. However, there is no chance of it waking up, as through its skull is a large steak knife accompanied by several stab wounds to the neck and back.

"I guess someone is here," Ray mutters quietly, stepping over the undead body.

"Might explain why it's so quiet," Tom replies, chiming in. This is their first dead body since the aquarium.

While Ray and the others press forward, Adrian lets go of her brother's hand to examine the knife in the undead patron's head. It has a red handle and a logo for the Whimsical Domain. Gripping the knife handle, she plucks it from the undead's head to take a closer look. It is definitely from a restaurant she helped Tyler raid.

"Everything okay, sis?" Steve asks as he stops to see what she's doing.

"Peachy", she replies, standing herself back up, holding onto the knife.

It is surprising to Adrian that Tyler might still be alive. In fact, the farther the group presses on, the more bodies appear on the trail. Two, four, ten undead patrons just completely butchered along the cobblestone. Each appears to have been taken out by different blades and knives. If this really is Tyler's work, he has indirectly helped the group by clearing a pathway and doing the hard work for them.

It isn't long before the pathway leads the group to a large opening in the park where jungle-themed shops and restaurants reside. To the right of the shops is the popular Wilderness Rapids ride, a lazy river-style ride where riders sit in the middle of a large circular boat that takes its riders through a jungle setting.

And just beyond the Wilderness Rapids ride, the monorail station.

Only problem: eight dozen undead patrons, possibly more, stand between them and their ticket out.

Chapter 18

A loud revving noise booms through the air. A cloud of dust fills the air as dirt is kicked up from a rapidly spinning wheel. A large, windowless, green Jeep with two seats up at the front and three rows of long bench-like seats behind recklessly plows through a large group of undead patrons. In the passenger seats, two teens.

Madi, an eighteen-year-old girl, is leaning out one side of the window with a large baseball bat, taking swings at any undead patrons and animals they passed. Her fiery red hair is tied into a long ponytail, which is threaded through a blue baseball cap, whipping in the wind.

Aaron, Madi's nineteen-year-old boyfriend, is throwing Molotov cocktails out the other side of the Jeep. Each one explodes on the ground and ignites whatever dead things they pass into flames. Aaron doesn't care if they are effective or not. It is just cool to be blowing shit up.

And, of course, foot pressed down on the gas and hands

gripping the steering wheel, is the driver, Tyler.

* * *

When the undead attack at the museum, Tyler does the only logical thing a person can do: run. And run he does. Thankfully, with the help of the chaos and noise from the museum, he slips out with little detection.

It is why he liked having a small group of people around. When trouble hit, it provided a scapegoat, allowing him time to make a move for it. Things didn't quite go as planned at the museum, but it worked out in the end.

While the undead patrons are distracted with the museum, Tyler bolts toward the Africa Pride Lands, a guided tour ride where educational facts are spewed at its riders while they gawk at what we can only assume are animals drugged out of their minds to appear more docile and not attack the busload of people. Because who needs animal rights when we can have a cute wildcat sleeping on the Jeep's roof?

It is here that Tyler meets up with Madi and Aaron. Just like Tyler, they have taken the offensive approach. The couple is just in the middle of hot-wiring a Jeep when Tyler arrives. Seeing that the three of them all have the same intention of just completely ruling this newly created zombie world, it makes sense that they team up, and like that, Tyler takes to the driver's seat and their adventure in "undead" hunting has begun.

* * *

Driving at full speed, the Jeep catches some air, flying out of the Africa Pride Lands and into the bazaar.

An undead woman stumbles toward the Jeep from the left side and, naturally, Tyler veers the Jeep toward her, hitting her with the left side door before her body is sucked under by the Jeep's spinning wheels. The undead woman releases a bloodcurdling squeal as the tire spins rapidly over her face, eventually crushing her skull and brains into nothing but a bloodied mess.

Tyler brings the Jeep into a donut as Aaron busts out his own baseball bat. Leaping from his seat, he hangs off the back of the Jeep as he attacks the undead patrons head on, while Madi is leaning out the window with a psychotic grin on her face as she swings her own bat.

* * *

"That's one way to clear a path," Tom says with a small smirk as he holds Aiden close to his chest, to keep him from viewing the killing spree happening ahead, just across from the Wilderness Rapids ride.

"They seem to be enjoying that a bit too much," Vanessa replies, doing the same thing with Joshua.

"If it clears us a path. Let them enjoy it," Ray replies as they all watch from a somewhat safe distance.

Once the undead are cleared, the Jeep swerves over to Ray and the group. Drifting to the side and stopping with a loud screech against the cobblestone, the Jeep is accompanied by the scent of burning rubber mixed with blood that fills the air momentarily.

"Need a lift?" Tyler says with a proud smirk on his face,

recognizing Tom and the others from the museum.

"Not with you," Vanessa replies, being a good mother and knowing that there is no way in hell she will ever subject her boys to that kind of recklessness.

"Let me drive, and we'll consider it," Ray says, chiming in and taking the lead, knowing that it will be the easiest way to get to their destination, but agreeing with Vanessa: there is no chance in hell he is going to allow some punk kid to chauffeur them around.

"We found this vehicle. Thus, we drive," Aaron adds, returning to his original seat in the Jeep, half leaning out the window. "There is plenty of room and, honestly, this is probably much safer than walking out in the open."

"Come on, they'd rather get themselves killed," Madi says with a whiny voice, moving beside Aaron and leaning on him with a bored yawn. "Let's just go. I'm getting tired."

Adrian lets out a sigh as she takes hold of her brother's hand. There are so many pros and cons to this whole situation. The redhead girl has a point. They have a vehicle, giving them an advantage against the undead patrons. You can store and carry more food and weapons with a car versus walking around with whatever bags you can carry. In the long run, having the Jeep seems like the safer choice for her brother and, in all fairness, she is getting bored. Though Tyler isn't the brightest bulb, he does keep things interesting.

"We're coming, too," Adrian states, pulling her brother along. The pros at the moment are outweighing the cons.

"Good luck," she calls out to Ray and the others as she and Steve board the Jeep.

Revving the engine twice, Tyler slams his foot on the

gas pedal. The wheels spin rapidly against the cobblestone before taking off at full speed through the park and toward the Jungle Experience, disappearing past the Wilderness Rapids ride where Madi and Aaron originally made their home base.

Chapter 19

The moment Tyler and his new groupies take off in the stolen park Jeep, Ray and the others step out into the open.

What used to be a small marketplace is now just a massive, bloody mess of crushed, mutilated bodies, with one particular group that is nearly impossible to tell where one person starts and another ends as their mangled corpses have been run over so many times that their flesh has practically become intertwined into one.

Cautiously, Ray takes the first step forward into the now-cleared bazaar. Behind him, Hannah follows, holding her shirt up over her face as the stench of death, decay, and rubber is almost too intense for her to handle. She gags a little as she tries not to think about the bodies she is stepping over, realizing it is nearly impossible not to step in blood or on what used to be a person.

Behind them, Vanessa, Tom, and the elderly man follow,

each watching their step.

"Disgusting," the elderly man mutters as he accidentally steps through a person's chest. He takes his foot out and kicks it to the side, removing a piece of lung that has stuck to his shoe as if he has just stepped in dog shit.

"You going to be okay?" Ray asks, noticing Hannah is turning a little green.

Hannah steps ahead of Ray, wanting to get through this bloodied mess as quickly as possible. She can just feel her stomach churning inside as she isn't the greatest with gross things like blood and dead bodies.

Unable to hold it anymore, Hannah spots a nearby garbage can. With her hand now completely over her mouth, she sprints over to the can. She places her hands on each side of the garbage can before leaning her head in and letting her meal from this morning all out.

Being the gentleman he is, Ray walks up behind Hannah. He awkwardly holds his hand onto her back and starts to gently rub it. "You're going to be alright," he says calmly, trying to assure Hannah that this response she is having is completely normal. "We're almost in the clear," he continues.

While most would find a girl puking into a garbage can disgusting, it actually reminds Ray of all the nights he spent with his daughter when she was sick. As much as throwing up sucks, there is nothing you can do other than allow the bug to pass. He can just see his little girl sitting in bed with her head in her own garbage can. It is absolutely disgusting, but this is what fathers deal with. Ray would sit behind her, comforting Bella during this horrible time by gently rubbing his daughter's back, assuring her they would to get through this together.

Hannah lets out one final dry heave before pulling herself up from the garbage can, having finally emptied her stomach's contents. Ray stops rubbing Hannah's back and stakes a step away to give her some space. "Better?" he asks, making sure that Hannah has got everything out of her system.

Hannah nods as she wipes her face with her shirt, seeing that she does not have a towel or anything else at the moment. "I'll be fine," she says with an embarrassed look on her face. "Thanks." Fully pulling herself away from the garbage, she notices a body that she initially missed lying against the trash can on the other side. Slowly, Hannah walks around to the other side of the bin, her heart sinking with each and every step as the body comes into full view.

The body is of a young male close to Hannah's age. He is wearing green cargo shorts, BIRKENSTOCK sandals and a white beater tip that has been torn to shreds. His chest has been completely ripped open; his rib cage is split open like a drawbridge. His right eye is bulging from his face.

A few moments ago, Hannah had her head in the garbage can because she could not deal with all the death around them, and now she is on her knees in front of a dead body with her hands wrapped around the body, pulling it into a very bloody embrace as she cries.

"Marcus, I'm so sorry!" she says as she rests his limp head on her shoulder, placing a hand against the back of his head, running her fingers through his hair, which is sticky and knotted with clots of blood.

Ray goes to say something but ends up biting his lip, unsure of what to say. He understands why she is upset. This is apparently her future husband. This is the person she was going to be starting a brand-new life with, having only accepted his proposal yesterday.

Standing by and watching the scene, Vanessa passes Joshua to Tom as she approaches Hannah. She crouches down to Hannah and gently places a comforting hand on her shoulder.

"I'm sorry for your loss," Vanessa says respectfully, knowing that if it were Tom in this situation, she too would be the same way.

Hannah hugs Marcus' dead body even more as she cries louder. She doesn't even care that she is covering her clothes in his blood. (Technically, her shirt is already covered in vomit). She barely notices Vanessa. Hannah is so stuck on the idea of her future husband being alive that she is not ready for this moment. "Leave me alone," she chokes out, not wanting to leave Marcus, even if he is dead.

Vanessa speaks softly to the grieving woman. "We're not leaving you behind."

"No," Hannah spits out between her sudden rush of emotions. "I'm not leaving Marcus! Not again!"

Listening in on this conversation, Ray decides maybe he should chime in. "Hannah, don't let Marcus' death be for nothing," Ray states firmly. "Just keep moving forward and live on for Marcus!"

"I have nothing left," Hannah begs, not wanting to move, as grief has completely immobilized her. "Just go."

"I'll stay with her!" the elderly man says, stepping

forward, speaking in a soft yet firm voice. "You folks go on, and we'll catch up."

While the old man is tired with this whole situation, he knows that if they try to pry her away, she will probably end up being more trouble for the group. And as much as he would have liked to just leave her behind, he can't pull himself to do it. She reminds him too much of his daughter.

"Is that alright with you?" Ray asks, turning his attention to Hannah. This whole time the old man \has been kind of quiet, so it is a bit of a surprise when he speaks up.

The old man approaches Hannah, crouching down beside her, just opposite Vanessa. "I came here with my kids and grandkids," he says, reaching into his wallet to pull out a photo of his family. "Michelle, my oldest. Peter, her husband, and their three kids, Junior, Stephanie, and Walter," he says, pointing to each person in the photo. "Yesterday was our last day at the park. We were supposed to be on a plane home a few hours ago." He pauses a moment and waves his hand to dismiss Vanessa and the others, mouthing for them to go on.

On the outside, the old man seems cold and uncaring, but inside? He knows exactly what Hannah is going through. He watched his son-in-law get brutally mauled to death. Junior, the oldest of the three grandchildren, faced the same unfortunate fate. As for Michelle and the other two kids? He doesn't know if they are dead or alive. They were separated in the crowds. But unlike Vanessa, who held onto hope, the old man has chosen not to get his hopes up and just accepts that they are all gone.

"It's just me now, and I understand the sadness building inside."

He chooses his words carefully, not wanting to come across as someone who has "lost more" but rather as someone who can help her get through this. Whether it is in his nature as a grandfather or the fact that Hannah reminds him a little of his own daughter, the elderly man decides that he will stay as long as needed.

"Maybe I should stay, too," Ray states, not wanting to leave the two of them alone. There is no way Hannah can protect herself, and he has no idea what the old man is capable of or if he can even protect her.

The old man turns his head to face Ray, almost insulted that Ray doesn't trust him to keep Hannah safe. Without any words, he waves the back of his hand to Ray, dismissing him.

"Just be careful," Ray adds, not wanting to argue with an old man.

"We'll see you on the other side," Vanessa adds as she returns to her husband, this time taking Aiden into her arms as he reaches out to his mommy.

"I'm hungry," Joshua whines.

"Me too. When can we eat?" Aiden adds as he wraps his arms around his mom's neck to hold on to her tightly.

"Mommy's hungry, too," she replies softly. "As soon as we get to COPET, we will find something to eat."

Each of them feels guilty about the idea of leaving their new friends behind, but it is the best option considering their situation. All they can do now is press forward and hope that Hannah and the old man will meet up with them.

The three adults continue forward toward the Wilderness Rapids line entrance, where they will find the pathway that leads past the ride and to the monorail station. The three of them completely disappear into the distance, leaving Hannah alone with the old man.

As Hannah holds the body of Marcus close, just completely lost in a world of sorrow, a low moan carries on the wind. A puddle of blood ripples as a dirtied and torn sneaker steps through it. The moan gets louder. A shadow stretches over the mangled bodies toward Hannah and the elderly man, who is sitting beside her with a hand on her shoulder.

Chapter 17

O f all the places that Tyler and his buddies can go to on their psychotic little killing spree, this is one area they have missed. Though the monorail is not far ahead of Ray and the others, the space between is filled with undead patrons as far as the eye can see. Most of them are probably victims who shared the same idea of escaping via the monorail, people funnelling into the station, succumbing to their panic as they pushed and shoved each other, trying to get through the doors, resulting in a bloody massacre of innocent lives.

"God damn it," Tom mutters as he sees the crowd before them, not even caring about swearing in front of his own child.

"We'll find another way," Vanessa adds, trying to be as optimistic about this whole situation.

"How? We aren't getting through that," Tom replies with frustration.

While Vanessa and Tom go back and forth between their thoughts, Ray's eyes wander. He examines the group ahead of them. Even with his stanchion, he can't take that group on. There really is no way forward, not unless they have a death wish. Silently, Ray's eyes leave the group toward one of the park's attractions: Water Rapid Adventure. A grin forms on Ray's face as he is struck with an idea. They don't have to fight their way through the undead horde. There is another way, and Ray has just figured it out.

"We don't have to get through that," Ray adds, giving Tom a look as he offers his stanchion to him. "Want to go for a ride?"

Chapter 18

A long stone walkway stretches through a forged forest with cheesy bird chirping sound effects and animatronic animals, which leads its riders toward two separate paths: entry and exit.

At the front of the entry line stands a large, hut-shaped pavilion with a wooden platform that constantly moves clockwise, allowing a smooth flow of riders getting in and out of the ride's round bumper boats.

In the centre of the rotating dock is the control panel, which is really used for those few times when people need assistance getting into the boats. The rest of the time, whoever oversees the ride just gets to sit around in the shade and relax.

Now, the ride itself is off. The water still flows upstream and around the ride, but the boats are all lined around the stationed dock and completely backed up. Minus the few bodies floating face down in the river and hanging off some of the tubes, the ride is clear.

"We're good!" Ray says, as he cautiously peers over several boats, holding a large tree branch he has picked up from the forested walkway to the ride.

"Let's do it!" Tom replies, tossing the stanchion Ray has handed him into the third tube back from the front.

As Tom hops into the boat, Ray approaches the ride's control panel and slams his hand down on the start button.

Click.

Click.

Click.

The gears move again. Within seconds, the dock turns, sending the first boat down into the river.

As the ride has been started up, Ray dashes from the control panel over to the boat where Tom is waiting. He jumps into the boat, taking a seat beside Tom as they both watch the next boat ahead get launched off.

"Not too late to back out," Tom says with a smirk. "Oh, you sure you don't want this?"

Tom holds up the metal stanchion, offering it back to Ray. Ray returns the smirk as he shakes his head and holds up the tree branch. "This is a bit more my weight," he replies with a small chuckle as he is very clearly comparing his slimmer physique to Tom's more muscular body.

Reaching the point of no return, Ray and Tom's boat reaches the end of the platform, sending them down the river. On its first turn, the boat bounces off the rock wall, sending it into a spin as it crashes into a wave of water, completely soaking Ray. Tom, who is sitting right beside him, remains mostly dry.

Tom can't help but laugh at the sight of Ray looking like a drowned rat. Hell, that is always the best part of the ride, as it is Russian roulette as to who is going to walk out drenched versus bone dry.

Lining the river are large cliffs with railings sitting atop for onlookers to tease and taunt the riders below. But now, there is nothing but undead patrons. Hundreds of them, all following the sound of the rushing water and crashing boats, just as planned.

As the boat approaches an underpass, Tom and Ray both go silent. Carefully, the two of them stand up in the ride. As the boat emerges from the other side, the two of them start screaming and yelling. Ray and Tom even reach into their pockets, removing small rocks they have picked up along the trail.

"Hey! Over here!" Ray yells out loudly as he throws the rock up toward the crowd of undead patrons.

The rock bounces off the rail, *pinging* as it hits the metal before landing on the ground, drawing the attention of five undead patrons.

Tom lets out a booming yell which echoes through the park before whipping his own a rock into the air. "This way, you fuckers!"

* * *

"How much longer?" Aiden asks as he tugs on Vanessa's arm.

"Can we please just go home?" Joshua plants his face into Vanessa's other arm before fully leaning on her. "I don't like it here!"

Vanessa lets go of Joshua's hand and slides hers across

his shoulders to his back as she gently rubs it in a circular motion. While she is listening to her boy's commentary about being hungry and missing their home, she keeps silent, her eyes focused ahead. Suddenly, a rock comes flying from below, pelting one of the undead patrons in the head, drawing its attention to the safety railing for the river ride below.

* * *

It doesn't take long for the undead patrons to take the bait. Several of them head right for the safety railing, tumbling over the cliff like lemmings and falling into the rapids below. One lucky patron lands in the boat directly behind Ray and Tom's. Its back snaps as it lands on the hard rubber surface. Its legs are in the ride while its head hangs over the edge into the water, only to be crushed into a bloody mess as the boat spins itself into the wall.

Tom and Ray sit back down in their boat as it continues into its final stretch. The two of them are relieved to see the plan working. Unfortunately, before they can celebrate, an undead patron emerges from the water below. As it attempts to climb into their boat, it reaches out to Ray. Its arm stretches out as Ray uses his tree branch to shove the creature away. As the boat crashes into a wall, Ray stumbles, stabbing the tree branch right into the undead patron's eye. As the boat spins, he accidentally pulls the stick back out of the patron. The undead patron falls into the water, floating face first, as it's tossed around in the red-tinted water. Ray lets out a small sigh of relief before noticing that like a marshmallow ready to be roasted, on the end of his branch is the eyeball belonging to the undead patron, complete with dangling optic nerve.

Ray lets out a small, startled scream as he sees what is accidentally left behind. Without even thinking, he holds the branch up to the side of the ride's walls, allowing the eyeball to smear itself along the rocks until it eventually comes off.

Farther along the ride, an undead patron hops the fence and, in perfect timing, lands in Ray and Tom's boat. With his quick action, Tom swings the stanchion just as the boat is approaching another wall with just enough spin to allow the strike to pin the undead patron between the stanchion and the ride's wall, the undead patron falling into the water as the boat drifts away.

The boat slows down as the end is near. It approaches a small ramp, where several other boats are patiently waiting to be set out. This is the end of the line. Ray and Tom both stand up in the boat, readying themselves to make an escape, until suddenly, an undead patron drops from the cliff above. It lands in the boat, and before anyone can react, it tackles Tom out of the boat and into the water.

"Shit! No!" Ray exclaims as he leans over the edge of the boat, smashing the branch into the undead patron's cranium repeatedly until it lets go of Tom. Finally, with another hit to the skull, the branch snaps in half, splintering into several shards, which Ray then stabs into the undead patron's face. The branch pieces pierce the undead patron's eyes, cheeks, and lips, resulting in a loud, mumbled moan as the undead stumbles back, eventually falling into the water, motionless.

"You okay?" Ray asks as he reaches over the boat's edge to help Tom back in.

"Yeah," Tom replies as he's pulled back in, and with perfect timing, too, because the boat behind them is just arriving back at the station. A few seconds later and he would have been a Tom sandwich.

With no time left to waste, Tom and Ray abandon their weapons, knowing they will only slow them down as they leap from their boat to the boat ahead.

Behind them, a boat comes from up the river, running over a few unsuspecting undead patrons that are having trouble getting through the water. The empty boat then swirls around, knocking another undead patron into the ride's wall. It is safe to say that this ride is the perfect choice for slowing them down.

Climbing over the boats, Tom and Ray return to the rotating platform where the ride begins. They both collapse onto the rotating dock, catching their breaths as large puddles of water form around them, slowly soaking the wooden dock.

Chapter 19

With a small smile on her face, Vanessa crouches down to her children's level. She pulls the twins in front of her and looks them both in the eyes. "Okay, on the count of three, we are going to have a race to that building over there," she states calmly, pointing toward the monorail station. The twins look at the building and then back at their mother. "Just pretend you're playing baseball; you've just hit the ball far, and that building is home. Let's go for that home run!"

The boys both give a nod as they take Vanessa's hands again.

Vanessa hates that she has to ask her boys to run alongside with her, but holding the two while trying to run will only slow the three of them down, making them more vulnerable than they already are.

As the undead start to clear the path, distracted by the noises from below, Vanessa begins her count.

One.

Two.

Three.

On the third count, Joshua and Aiden take off running, keeping close to each other while Vanessa slows her pace to keep close behind them, keeping her eyes focused on everything around them.

Mid run, Aiden's shoes kick up some gravel, drawing the attention of a patron located from the back of the crowd. It gives a low growl as it directs its attention to the twins, breaking away from the group of other undead.

Seeing this sudden change in movement, Vanessa speeds up her pace. She holds out her elbow and braces herself as she body slams herself into the undead patron and through, knocking it down to the ground as she continues past.

Just a few feet from the door and another stray undead patron emerges. It reaches out for Joshua with bloodthirsty eyes. From behind, Vanessa goes into a sprint, throwing herself between Joshua and the undead patron like a football player trying to protect the quarterback. With her arm stretched out straight, she clotheslines the undead patron.

Now ahead of the twins and with no time to stop, Vanessa runs into the door of the monorail station. She slams right into it, the door opening inwards upon impact. She quickly steps into the building, holding the door open for her boys to pass. Behind the twins is the first undead patron that was knocked down, now back on its feet and determined to get its prey. The boys rush through the door as Vanessa forces it closed. The undead patron crashes into the door, its face pressed firmly on the glass. Streaks of blood and spit are smeared across the glass as it pulls its head off and begins banging on the door, as if it were demanding to be let in. Vanessa stands there with her back pressed firmly against the other side. Her heart races as the door jolts with every hit from the undead patron.

Trembling, Vanessa places her hand against the door, sliding her fingers along the glass until she can feel the handle. From there, she feels around until she finally finds it. The lock. She locks the door as she continues to hold her weight against the door, afraid to move. Her heart pounds against her chest.

Bang.

Bang.

Bang.

Just when Vanessa is fearing for the worst, positive it is going to break through the glass, the undead patron stops, peeling its face from the glass as it turns its attention elsewhere. Carefully, Vanessa turns herself around slightly to see what is happening outside. As it walks away, she lets out a small sigh of relief.

Relaxing her legs, Vanessa leans back against the door as she slowly slides until she is seated on the ground.

"Come here," Vanessa says quietly to her boys as she catches her breath, stretching her arms out to them. "Come here . . ."

Joshua and Aiden don't have to be asked twice. The moment they see their mother holding her arms out for a hug, they have already moved in. Picking their own sides, they take a seat and snuggle beside her. Vanessa gives a gentle squeeze as she kisses each boy on the top of the head. "You boys are so brave," she says, leaning her head back and closing her eyes as she catches her breath.

Chapter 20

Tom and Ray aren't that far behind Vanessa. The two of them are both completely running on adrenalin as they swerve around undead patrons, jump over dead bodies, and sprint like their lives depend on it. Because their lives do depend on it.

With most of the undead patrons distracted by the ride, the only thing standing between Tom, Ray, and the door is the undead patron trying to break through the glass. Its attention is pulled from the door to the two men charging in its direction. As Ray shows down, Tom speeds up and braces himself like a football player. He plows right through the undead patron, slamming it back into the door. The loud *thud* grabs the attention of Vanessa, who practically leaps from her skin at the sudden noise.

Seeing who is on the other side, Vanessa gets up with haste. She unlocks the door as her husband steps over the downed undead patron to enter the building.

A few seconds later, Ray comes running with a few more undead patrons following behind. As he approaches the door, his right foot plants itself through the undead patron's head like he is stomping on a pumpkin. The gooey insides cause Ray to lose his footing as he ungracefully trips his way through the door, landing on his face.

As Ray is in the clear, Tom pushes the door closed, locking it as quickly as possible. And just in time, too, as the patrons behind Ray run right into the door like birds flying into a freshly cleaned window.

Taking a small step back, Tom keeps his eyes on the door. He leans forward, tapping the glass on his side with his knuckles. While he isn't an expert, he will have to say that it is probably hurricane-proof glass or something close.

Confident that the door is going to hold, Tom turns his attention to Ray with a smirk. "You really stuck that landing!" Tom says with a chuckle as he extends his hand to help Ray back to his feet.

Ray stands up with the help of Tom, rolling his eyes at the joke. "Ha. Ha," he replies flatly.

As Ray dusts himself off, Vanessa practically leaps onto Tom. She wraps her arms around his neck as she plants a passionate kiss on his lips. She had faith in her husband, believing that this will work out in the end, but there had also been that sinking feeling deep down that they weren't going to see each other again.

"Shall we see if the monorail is working?" Vanessa asks as she pulls away from Tom, turning toward the stairs just up ahead that lead to the platform.

As Vanessa walks toward the stairs, Joshua and Aiden run

to their dad. "You boys are so brave," Tom says as he play-fully squeezes them. "Thank you for keeping Mommy safe!"

Joshua and Aiden giggle as they each pick a side and take their dad's hand. The three of them follow Vanessa.

As Tom passes by Ray, a small rip in Tom's shirt, just under his left shoulder blade catches Ray's attention. It is hard to tell at first, as his shirt is still wet, but there are three lines torn through his shirt, about the size of a male hand, with blood seeping through. Ray feels his chest tighten. It is possible he just got caught on something, but chances are this is from when Tom was pulled into the water. They were both in such a panic that it was possible he didn't even notice or feel anything penetrate his skin.

"Tom, take off your shirt," Ray chokes out, as Tom is halfway up the stairs.

"What?" Vanessa replies with confusion in her voice.

Tom turns around in confusion. He sees the concern on Ray's face as he then looks to his shoulder and tugs on his shirt, noticing the bloodstains and rips through it. He pales as he completely removes his shirt.

From the front, he is a very fit man with a perfectly chiselled chest, like something you'd see in a magazine. Just the absolute image of perfection. On his back, also perfectly sculpted, are three long, bleeding scratches that no doubt have been formed by a human hand. Or what used to be a human hand. Most likely from the last undead patron they encountered, when he recklessly tackled the creature into the door.

Chapter 21

Vanessa, Tom, Aiden, and Joshua are sitting inside one of the "cleaner" cars of the monorail, which isn't really by much as they all are decorated with blood and bodies (some of which are reanimated and forever trapped inside the small metal prisons). This one just has the least number of bodies.

The family just sits there, both boys sitting on their dad's lap as he quietly bounces them on his knee while Ray allows them some space, waiting outside on the platform, trying to figure out a way to get the monorail going.

Tom forces a smile as he starts to come to terms with the fact that his time is nearly up. Joshua and Aiden mean the world to him and all he has ever wanted is to be there. Watch them grow up, start school, graduate, go off to college, get married. The twins have their whole lives ahead of them, and the thought of himself not being there completely breaks Tom's heart. Not to mention Vanessa, his beautiful wife. They are supposed to get through this hell together. He promised her they would. Tom's eyes water as he pulls the boys into a hug. "I want you both to be good for your mother, you hear me?" he chokes out as he gives a kiss on each of their cheeks.

"You know we're good!" they both reply with innocent grins on their faces, neither of them fully aware that this is the last time they are going to see their dad. A decision made by both Tom and Vanessa to keep them from getting too worked up.

Tears roll down Tom's eyes as he lifts each boy off his lap. He feels his muscles tensing inside as the virus is taking its effect. Beads of sweat drip down his face as he struggles to keep his humanity just a little longer. He takes in a deep breath, holding it a moment before letting it out and speaking. "I love you both."

"Why don't you go see if Ray needs help?" Vanessa says as she places her hands on the twins' backs, giving them a little push out of the car.

As soon as they exit, Vanessa turns her attention back to her husband. As much as she tries to hold it together, Vanessa finally just lets the tears out as she gets closer to Tom, placing her warm hands on his cold, wet cheeks.

"I'm so sorry . . ." Tom chokes out, trying to hold on just a little more as the world in front of him becomes shrouded in a dark haze. "I lo-ve you . . . so . . ."

Vanessa closes her eyes momentarily as she leans in and places her soft lips against her husband, pulling him into one final loving embrace, knowing that words are unnecessary.

As she pulls away from the kiss, Vanessa gazes into her

husband's once-bright blue eyes, now completely dull and grey. The life in Tom's eyes is completely gone, even though tears continue to flow down.

"I love you, too," she says quietly as she tightens her grip on Tom's face. Vanessa bites down on her lip as she breathes in deeply through her nose. Her heart is just pounding in her chest as she stands there trembling, knowing what she has to do but unsure if she can. Closing her eyes, Vanessa lets out her breath as she twists Tom's head to the side in one swift motion. Tom's body instantly goes limp as the sound of a bone cracking echoes in Vanessa's ears.

As Tom's body drops, Vanessa carefully adjusts it across the seats in the monorail car, pulling his eyes closed. She stands over Tom's body as hers continues to tremble. The grief builds inside as she holds back the urge to just scream.

Vanessa takes several deep breaths in and out, using the breathing techniques learned from her Yoga classes to try to control her emotions. In and out. Finally, she gives Tom one last kiss goodbye.

"Let's go," Vanessa says with very little emotion as she exits the car.

"You sure you're ready?" Ray asks, as the boys each leave Ray's side and return to their mom's side.

Vanessa silently nods as she tries her best to hold it all in, the voice in her head telling her she has to remain strong. She has to do it for the boys. It sucks, but she has to keep going, even if a piece of her has just died. And she thinks holding it all in will be easy, until the boys speak.

"Isn't Daddy coming with us?"

"I want to hold Daddy's hand!"

As the words leave the twins' lips, Vanessa finds herself unable to hold it in. She promised Tom that she wouldn't tell the boys the truth until they were safe, but she quickly realizes it won't be possible. This is something she can't hide from her boys.

"No, Daddy's not coming with us," she finally says, unable to hold it all in. She shakes her head as she becomes blinded by the tears, unable to make them stop. Vanessa drops to her knees as she pulls her boys in close to her, holding them tightly.

"I'm so sorry!"

Chapter 22

The sun is setting as the day is coming to its end.

Tyler, Adrian, Steve, Madi, and Aaron all sit around a small campfire in the middle of the African Pride Lands with meats from various animals cooking on sticks over the fire. The group is just laughing and having fun, as if they are enjoying a normal camping experience. That is, if a normal camping experience includes sitting in the middle of an artificial desert with countless dead bodies scattered around the campers.

Over by the bazaar, Marcus' body leans against the garbage can, as the body of the elderly man rests a few feet away while an undead patron wearing sequined squirrel ears is leaning over his body, making a snack of his intestines. No sign of Hannah to be seen.

Finally, at the monorail station, all power to the trains is out due to the wires being severed, leaving Ray and Vanessa no choice but to make the trek to COPET on foot. As the twins are exhausted, Ray carries Joshua while Vanessa takes Aiden. The two of them carefully make their way along the narrow monorail track, venturing out toward the unknown world ahead of them as the sun disappears, bringing them into darkness.

Epilogue

Back at the market, Hannah holds the body of Marcus close, completely lost in a world of sorrow. A low moan carries on the wind. A puddle of blood ripples as a dirtied and torn sneaker steps through it. The noise of death gets louder. A shadow stretches across mangled bodies toward Hannah and the elderly man, who is sitting beside her with a hand on her shoulder.

To be continued . . .

9 781039 184336